UNREGULATED CHICKEN BUTTS

UNREGULATED CHICKEN BUTTS

AND OTHER STORIES BY
ILYAS HALIL

Selected and Translated by
JOSEPH S. JACOBSON

University of Utah Press — Salt Lake City
1990

Copyright © 1990 University of Utah Press
All rights reserved

∞ The paper in this book meets the standards for
permanence and durability established by the
Committee on Production Guidelines for Book Longevity
of the Council on Library Resources

Library of Congress Cataloging-in-Publication Data

Ilyas Halil.
  [Short stories. English. Selections]
  Unregulated chicken butts and other stories / Ilyas Halil ;
selected and translated by Joseph S. Jacobson.
    p.   cm.
  Selected stories from the author's Doyumsuz göz and Çiplak Yula.
  ISBN 0-87480-349-7 (pbk : alk. paper)
  I. Jacobson, Joseph S.   II. Title.
PL248.H225A6   1990
894'.3533—dc20   90-52742
                                          CIP

To
Irene,
Monica, Karen, Katya, and Marissa

CONTENTS

Introduction	3

————— **From *Doyumsuz Göz*** —————

Engineer Wanted	5
Humble Fehmi Bey	11
Discontent	17
Chinese Tuey	23
Chicken Thief	27
Living Cheap	31
No One to Yell at	35
Strikes	39
Computers	43
Unregulated Chicken Butts	49
Modest Livelihood	53
Turk in the Neighborhood	57
The Old Eskimo	63
Suicide in New York	69

————— **From *Çiplak Yula*** —————

Mill Street Strike	75
Agaluk	81
Montreal . . . Montreal . . .	85
Desert	89
Three Drunks in the Park	93
Spring in Magog	97
Chamberpot Music	101
Sniffles Rejep	107
Weather Science	115
Paleface	121
Anyone Want a Million Dollars?	127
Fat Tom	133
Naked Yula	141
Autumn in Montreal	147
Eagle-eye	151
Ingratitude	155

Doctor Ismail Düzer	161
Flying Birds	167
Roots	171
Mud	175
Morning Traffic	179

UNREGULATED CHICKEN BUTTS

INTRODUCTION

UNREGULATED CHICKEN BUTTS and Other Stories by Ilyas Halil presents thirty-five selected stories from *Doyumsuz Göz* and *Çiplak Yula* (*Dissatisfaction* and *Naked Yula*). Ilyas Halil's tales of the New World are exciting to Turkish readers, to whom America itself is fanciful. They enjoy the reading experience as Halil swings them back and forth on a satirical ride between realism and fantasy. Though these stories, selected by the author and me, were written for a Turkish audience, we believe they will excite the interest both of North Americans and of others who read English.

Born in Adana, Turkey, in 1930, Ilyas Halil attended public schools and spent his youth in Mersin. The stories comprising this anthology were written in Canada, where the author immigrated in 1964. His writing reveals his keen delight in describing the plight of people living in the advanced technological milieu of the New World. His mode of narration is basically satirical but spiced now and then with fantasy. The dilemma generated by imbalances in production and consumption in advanced economic systems stimulates some of his best humor, as you will see in "Unregulated Chicken Butts," "Discontent," and "Humble Fehmi Bey."

My esteemed readers should remember that the original stories have a Turkish audience, whose members, although appreciative of many occidental values, belong to a traditionally oriental culture. Nevertheless, I found no evidence in the original Turkish of intentional slur or innuendo against race, color, sex, or any specific group. In preparing the English version, I tried to maintain the author's neutral language in this respect. If any word or expression in this translation appears offensive, it was not so in the original Turkish, and was only used when more neutral language resulted in significant loss of literary fiber.

―――――――――― **Introduction** ――――――――――

In *World Literature Today,* the erudite Talat S. Halman, who introduced me to Ilyas Halil, reviews *Doyumsuz Göz* in the Winter 1984 issue: "In . . . his first collection of short stories, Halil emerges as a first-rate satirist who paints a chiaroscuro human comedy with a few rapid brush strokes. It is amazing how masterfully he squeezes slices of life into these miniscule stories (the longest is barely 1,500 words) and even more astonishing how they collectively and cumulatively offer the reader a tragicomic panorama of modern life. . . . Halil's satiric strategies extend from jeu d'esprit to black comedy to mordant indictment. His stories alternate between translucent whimsy and devastating condemnation of injustice, but the style is always wry and mild, often representing the best features of irony and never lacking in humanistic care."

One story from this anthology, "Engineer Wanted," first appeared in *Short Story International.* I must further acknowledge that the quality of my translations has been significantly enhanced by suggestions from my wife, Viola, a talented short-story writer in her own right. Though other works have been published by university presses, Turkish literature in English translation is comparatively rare and until now there has been no anthology in English from the gifted Ilyas Halil.

Fluent in Arabic and English, as well as his native Turkish, this endowed writer tells his stories of the new world as seen through the eyes of a Canadian immigrant particularly sympathetic toward swarthy, fellow Mediterranean types who have also come west to joust with mighty machines, tricky computers, and weird New World values concerning production and consumption. His strong interest in Native American Indians reveals sympathy for their conflicts with technologically advanced civilization.

The author is bewitched by art, artists, and fantasy. Don't be surprised when his realism suddenly turns to reverie! Sympathy for the little man endures, even as he points out his faults and foibles. Ilyas Halil's fresh view, of both Turkey and the New World, makes reading him a rewarding adventure.

Joseph S. Jacobson
Professor Emeritus

ENGINEER WANTED

I chanced across him in a metro station. He was a man of medium height with a slight paunch. His eyes shone with joy. At one look, you could instantly tell he was one of us, that is, a Mediterranean type. His face was a sunburned mixture of sea, mountains, and seaweed. He stopped. "Do you see these people?" he asked. "They all came here looking for work." I gave him a quizzical look and asked, "Who are you talking about?" He indicated the passengers getting off the subway train. "All of these people are following me; they all want me to give them a job. See that man in front wearing the green jacket? He's followed me all the way from Rome! 'We have no jobs!' I say. None of them listen. 'Please, brother, if you really want to, you can do it!' they answer. I beg your pardon, my friend, my name is Düzcan Şenkir. When I saw the Cumhurriyet newspaper in your hand, I knew you were one of us. I just returned to Canada from Turkey. If I don't tell someone about it, I'll explode from frustration."

He shook my hand. The man had the look of a joker. I couldn't determine whether or not what he said was true. Walking beside him, I listened.

Three weeks ago, no one in this world was happier than I. Now, after ten years, I was going on a trip to Turkey. What pleasure! I was going to steal three weeks from fate. I would eat the most splendid fish in Istanbul. In Bursa I would eat peaches, in Nigde, apples, in Mersin, oranges, in Adana, kebabs. Inside and out, I was overjoyed. This little stomach of mine, you see! The little devil kept on doing a belly dance all on its own! It ignored the traffic cops and danced wildly in the streets. It was as if the nation were playing a belly-dance tune and keeping time in my belly. A week before leaving, I started to diet. When I arrived, I was going to gulp down the most delicious, the richest food. I began longing for that excellent raki. Reach out, beauteous Turkey, give me your hand, my beloved homeland! I was ready to dive into Istanbul like a lover hopping into bed with his sweetheart. I dreamed about it every night.

An hour before I boarded the plane, my boss said, "If you can, find a good engineer for us while you're in Turkey, hire him. We just haven't been able to find a suitable engineer here." "Very well," I replied. Oh, if only I hadn't said that, if only I had held my tongue! Did I know what trouble it was going to get me into?

The day after we landed in Istanbul, I gave an ad to two newspapers announcing that we had an opening for an engineer to work in Canada at a good salary. Around evening, I returned to the hotel. As soon as I came in the door, the desk clerk said, "Seven people want to see you; I took them all to the waiting room." Seven people? Lord God, how quickly my friends and relatives heard I had arrived!

Happily, I rushed to the salon. Inside there wasn't a face I recognized. The clerk said, "Here are the gentlemen awaiting you." A middle-aged, fatherly man approached me, saying, "I learned that you need an engineer to work in Canada." "Where did you hear this?" I asked. "From my brother-in-law who works at the paper. Actually, your ad will appear tomorrow, but I thought I'd better see you today. What else could I do? It's a job! If I didn't act quickly they'd snatch it right out of my hand." Pointing to the six men beside him, I asked, "Are these your friends?" "No, sir, I don't know these gentlemen." Then the six others suddenly joined in the conversation. They all talked at once. I understood that all six were engineers and all wanted the job. They had learned of the ad in advance and had come to see me. One was saying, "I learned of your ad from the doorman at the newspaper. The bastard took me for a hundred lira." Another said, "Have you ever heard of such a shyster? So the low-down scoundrel sold the same ad to all six of us! There're sure a lot of greedy people in the world today!" Another, "Don't slander the poor guy! I bought the ad from the typesetter. Your doorman was generous. That damn typesetter took me for two hundred bucks. If it worked, I was ready to say, 'Take it with my blessing!' "

"Just a second, gentlemen, Leave your names and addresses. I'll get in touch with you tomorrow and invite you for an interview," I said.

That first day, the telephone rang nonstop until midnight. It rang itself off the hook. Before the ad was even published in the paper, nearly thirty people had applied. I gave them all appointments for the following day.

The next day, the ad appeared. If only it hadn't! All Istanbul had become populated with engineers! I woke up early that morning. After I had breakfast in my room, exactly at seven, the hotel manager appeared. "Please, sir," he said, "since five o'clock the hotel has been flooded with engineers looking for work. See these men as soon as possible so we can get back to our work. Actually, because of you, all the rooms in the hotel have been rented, but our employees can't cope with all the guests. If you would only go out and deal with them! They've even formed a line out in front waiting for you."

I looked out the window. A long line!

Inside, the hotel salon looked like the waiting room of a health clinic. People with sad, tired faces filled the room.

That day I interviewed no fewer than sixty people. The applicants all appeared to be competent engineers. Each had a good job. When I told them how difficult the work was on the job the firm proposed and how harsh the climate, the applicants' desire only grew. Though I emphasized the exhausting nature of the work, they still wouldn't get off my back.

That night I flopped into bed. From all the talking I had done, my tongue was swollen like an eggplant. I had three uncles and their children in Adana; in Kozan, my sister and her husband; in Bursa and Ankara, uncles; in Kayseri and Izmir, classmates. At least I could telephone friends and relatives and ask how they were! I asked the operator to get me Adana, Kozan, Bursa, Ankara, Kayseri, and Izmir.

Those who had called the first day and couldn't get an appointment raided the hotel in person early the next. I awoke to a hotel in tumult. Early morning, even before the rooster had a chance to crow, close to two hundred men were waiting in the street. A hot *salep* drink vendor and one selling *simit* rolls had set up their stands in the street and were doing a booming business with these new clients.

The hotelkeeper rushed up to my room. "Please, brother, come look at this!" he said. "Some have come, bag and baggage. Some have reserved seats on the plane. And they're not all engineers! Some are carpenters, some ironworkers, some cooks! 'Well,' the men say, 'where they have engineers, carpenters are needed.' The cooks are saying, 'With this many men, they probably need someone to cook their food.' And the barber from the corner left a customer with his face lathered and ran up saying, 'Hey now, if the cook's going, why shouldn't I?' I beg of you, sir! Go out and say something to these people! Pretty soon the whole town will move in here. They'll wreck my hotel."

Bewildered, I went out. "Those who are not engineers, don't wait!" I said. The crowd answered all together, "Don't we count, sir? Whenever you look at a construction site where there're engineers, there're always carpenters and ironworkers!" Although I told them, "There's only an opening for one engineer," no one listened to me and they stayed nailed to the spot where they stood.

Until noon the applicants didn't give me a chance to catch my breath. In the meantime, eight people applied by telephone from Hakkari, Urfa, Kars, Izmir, and Trabzon. By noon I was exhausted from fatigue and hunger. Moreover, I really had to go. I'll go wash my hands, I thought, but it was impossible to get out the door. The corridor was jammed with people. Some were talking, some were playing cards, and some had dozed off with their eyes closed. If these were all engineers, every construction site in Turkey must be closed. As soon as I stuck my head out the door, they all attacked me. Everyone was talking. Pushing and shoving, like a man swimming for land, I started making my way toward the toilet. Stroke by stroke I came nearer. As I battled the waves, the people tried to tell me their stories. They had worked five years with the Water Department, three years with the Highways, four at the Etibank, three at the Dams, in Germany, in France. They didn't want to miss out on the job in Canada. I would soon soil my pants.

Engineer Wanted

Somebody close beside me grabbed my hand. "Come, brother, you come with me! I'll take care of your problem!" he said. Oh, God bless you! There are still charitable people in the world! He took me by the hand and shoved me through a door. "Go in and relieve yourself!" he said. He locked the door from the outside. Inside it was dark. It was a Turkish-style toilet. There was someone inside. Saying to him, "I beg your pardon," I tried to leave. "Wait, sir! I've waited hours for you here!" the inside occupant said. "I'm an engineer. I was going to apply for the job in Canada but I just couldn't get you on the telephone. I'm in a hurry; I'm getting married tomorrow. I have no time to lose! You've got to come to the toilet sometime, I figured. The man waiting outside is my uncle. Sir, if you don't grant me an interview now, my uncle won't open the door! Go ahead, relieve yourself! I don't consider myself a stranger. After all, we're colleagues!"

We had the interview in the toilet. The next day, the hotelkeeper evicted me. That morning I slapped my things together and rushed outside. I hopped into a taxi standing at the door. "Quick, to the airport!" I told the driver. He turned to me and said, "So you're running away now? Aren't you ashamed? After giving all that hope to people, you run away like a thief in the night! Phui on you! There's no love for your country or people left in you!"

I sat where I was, shaking like a leaf. When I came to the airport, I saw that the place was surrounded by police. I thought the president of some foreign country must have arrived. As I looked stupidly around me, flashbulbs started popping everywhere. I was encircled by reporters. They rained questions on me. "You're hiring a hundred fifty engineers for Canada, right?" "Are you going to sign a labor agreement between Turkey and Canada?" "What in Turkey do Canadians like most?" Meanwhile, the police were trying to hold back the people trying to get at me. "Which food do you like the most?" "How is life in Canada?" "Do you miss your homeland?"

On the first flight, I went to Rome. Someone in a green jacket met me there. The man introduced himself, saying, "I am the Mersin Cemetery Director, Reşit!" He was looking for work and asked if I could help him. That's the last I remember; I had passed out!

When I opened my eyes, I was in Montreal.

HUMBLE FEHMI BEY

On his last visit, Fehmi Bey told us this story. I don't know if any of you know him. He's a short, quiet, respected person, an old Ottoman gentleman. He avoids getting involved with anyone. If he were in the same room with you, you wouldn't be aware he existed unless you wanted to use the chair he was sitting in. A humble person! They had formerly called him Humble Fehmi Bey in the place where he worked. Then they forgot the Fehmi and he became simply Humble Bey. Those who had recently come to the office didn't know his real name. A few years after he began work, the General Directorship even listed him as Humble Bey on the payroll. Fehmi Bey suffered considerable trouble because of this. Some places his name was documented as Fehmi Bey and others as Humble Bey. The confusion that arose in public offices dealing with marriage, death, deeds, and military service distressed him greatly. The Army Draft Board didn't look for him until he was thirty. But after he was thirty, they tried to make him do his military service twice.

The greatest mixup occurred when his daughter, Aysel, was married. At that time, Fehmi Bey was the Document Registration Clerk in the Recorder's office. He was living in a little three-room house with a rather large yard, which his late father had built in Küçükesat. In 1954, he was earning almost three hundred fifty lira. This was considered a lot of money, especially when he didn't have to pay rent every month. Thus Fehmi Bey was living with his beautiful daughter, Aysel, as an untroubled, quiet man, with no turmoil other than his name. That is, until the day Aysel became acquainted with the American, Sergeant Andrews.

After this acquaintance, Fehmi Bey's life fell into complete disarray. In short, his life lost all its flavor. Sergeant Andrews, whom

Humble Fehmi Bey

they called Andy, was a redheaded, freckled young man of twenty-three. He laughed a lot. He had white teeth. Like all the other Americans, he was generous with all the girls. He worked at one of the military missions in Kavaklidere. His salary was two thousand lira.

I don't recall how Andy and Aysel met, but I do know how Fehmi Bey's life became miserable. The American Embassy began an investigation concerning Fehmi Bey and his daughter. The secret inquiry continued a long time. Fehmi Bey faced all the questioning with a secretive smile. He submitted! He opposed nothing; he didn't rebel. Finally, in 1959, permission was granted for Andy and Aysel to marry. The young couple married and emigrated to America.

The now "Mister" Humble sold his house and all his property, converted the few lira that he received into dollars on the black market, and moved to Canada to live. Originally, he wanted to go to America, but they wouldn't give him a visa. He bought a house in a nice neighborhood in Montreal and settled in. His daughter lived in a town not too far away. Whenever it came into his head, he hopped on the bus and went to see her.

He became acquainted with his neighbors and even found himself a girl friend. The one I called a girl was a fifty-year-old plump German woman. Organizing a nice wedding attended by the whole neighborhood, he took the German woman home as his bride.

During the first weeks, the woman walked her dog every morning. She bathed him and prepared his food as well. However, the dog snarled viciously at Mr. Humble. He mumbled, "*Lahavle*, God give me strength!" Even though Mr. Humble complained about the dog a few times to his wife, it was of no use.

In his unhappiness, he concentrated on his job, working day and night, always doing his best. Mr. Humble worked in the accounting department of a factory that manufactured toilet paper. His industry was clearly evident. In a short time he became familiar with the factory inside and out. As he knew little English, he spent no time in idle chatter with others. He bought books on the production and sale of toilet paper and read them each evening until midnight to obtain information concerning the marketing of toilet tissue. With knowledge came efficiency, and promotion accelerated during this period. All the factory personnel admired this Turk. He spoke very little but smiled often.

First he became Assistant Accountant, then Director of Accounting. Within three years, the General Directorship of the factory passed into his hands. After acquiring the General Directorship, Mr. Humble became even more enterprising on the job. Factory sales grew fast; the percentage of profit rose. Under Mr. Humble's administration, the factory started production of colored toilet paper. The man who opened the market for toilet tissue with pictures of nudes for the male chauvinist trade was again Mr. Humble. After the toilet paper with the naked pictures was offered for sale, Mr. Humble's star shone brilliantly. Factory sales increased 300 percent. Profits began flowing like water.

Mr. Humble left the General Directorship and took over the chairmanship of the factory's Board of Directors. During this phase, the number of factories grew from two to seven. Fawn brand toilet paper became firmly established in the Canadian market. Then the factory's products found markets in all of America. Eventually no one was being wiped by any other paper. Mr. Humble produced different kinds of paper for everyone's needs. For the ladies, pleasant-pink, canary-yellow, honeydew-flesh, fresh-cashew-colored Fawn brand designer paper, and for those with socialist leanings he made red paper with a sickle.

However, the sales results were contrary to those expected. Democrats and Republicans used the red paper with the sickle, prepared especially for socialists, as an insult to them. And the tissue made for extremists sold mostly in workingmen's circles. After receiving this unexpected response, Mr. Humble had "KU KLUX KLAN" printed on toilet paper he manufactured for sale to the opponents of Klanism.

Within three or four years, the shy, humble man we had known became a rich Canadian. Everything he touched turned to gold.

One day, I asked him how such a quiet man could be so successful. "Very simple!" he replied. "There's nothing these Canadians and Americans won't buy! All you have to do is present a new product. They admire anything different or avant-garde. These consumers, whom we consider so stupid, are smarter than any of us. They know that if you don't take the money from them, the cogs of the entire system will stop and corrode. Canadians are aware of this. Therefore, they spend willingly and knowingly. Money left in the pocket is unproductive. For example, look at the new products I plan to manufacture next year. I'll bring scented toilet paper on the market for the first time. Then I'll produce paper of a thickness matching a person's skin and complexion. We've broadened our business program. Seven professors have been employed to conduct research on the subject. We intend to examine people's toilet habits, learn what they think about at that time, whom they curse, whom they are angry with, and produce tissue accordingly.

"I don't know if you listen to the radio. We propose to broadcast special music on radio stations to insure the loosening of people's bowels so they'll use the toilet every morning without fail. We've earmarked three million dollars to pay authorized individuals for this. According to our computations if people regularly have a bowel movement once each day, our paper sales will increase three times, resulting in a full 700 percent rise in profits. There's a lot of money in this business. For example, we've observed that the thing Americans worship most and also hate most is money. Therefore, our sales of rolls with pictures of one-hundred-dollar bills printed on them are brisk. In the United States, there are customers who finish a roll at one sitting. They come out of the toilet feeling as if they struck it rich."

In three years, Mr. Humble increased the number of Fawn factories from seven to eighteen. With the profits, he acquired a major portion of America's and Canada's industry, including steel mills and even soda-pop plants. The General Directors of all the factories gathered once a week to make their reports to Mr. Humble.

Then came 1974, a year filled with economic crises. Fawn toilet paper sales fell by half. It was agreed that Fawn factories must be closed in June due to the great loss.

Mr. Humble called a meeting of his Board of Directors. He presented for the Board's approval a remedy he'd devised through his expertise. In short, Mr. Humble made the following proposal:

"The decrease in sales could be turned around by mixing a little laxative into the products sold by our soda-pop factories. Insuring the softening of Canadian and American bowels will increase the sales of Fawn toilet paper. If we attain success, it will prevent unemployment and protect public health!"

The Board of Directors, accepting this proposal unanimously with applause, decided to put it into effect. . . .

DISCONTENT

I didn't use to be like this. I was a well-behaved, good man. Now, in spite of my cross-eyes and fifty-plus years, my shortened neck and big head, I have a passion for wearing new clothes, changing shoes, and sticking a fresh red carnation in my lapel every day. I confide to young girls, the age of my daughter, that I'm in love. God, and everybody else, knows I really can't carry off being a young blood. I always get smeared playing this game! Something goes wrong every time!

I please myself, I buy what I want from the shops and bring it home. After using it a couple of times, plop, into the trash can it goes. No matter what I do, it doesn't work; that wild creature inside me is never satisfied. In the years before I emigrated from Turkey to Canada, I wasn't this greedy. I remember the years when I worked at the Mersin Deeds office; once in six years I bought a new suit. For three years I wore it with one side out, then I had the cloth reversed and wore it three more with the other side showing. Still we were happy with our lives. "Thank God!" we used to say.

Anyway, it happened after we immigrated here. We started by trying to keep up with the neighbors. Upon returning home in the evening, before I could say, "Hello, dear, what's new?" crying, weeping her heart out, my wife started to complain, "Words fail me! You know that Italian woman across the street? She bought herself a new dress. It looks so good, oh so good on her! She stayed out all day. If a dried-up woman can dress that beautifully, why can't I? Just think about it! But I don't have a chance! I fell into the hands of a man like you, who doesn't know the value of women. Just look at these Canadian couples! The guys fulfill their wives' every desire. The men always do the dishes and laundry. If you ask why, it's in order to

Discontent

keep the women's hands beautiful and young! Until evening, the wives gallivant around. What's more, they're ugly as sin. Bags of bones! A dog would choke on them! Oh, poor unlucky me!"

From now on at home it's nagging every night. On one side my wife, on the other the children. As if the damn family has stopped work and spied on the neighborhood all day! The neighbor bought this, let's us hurry and buy one. The neighbor ate that, come on, let's us have the same dish. If I say, "Wait just a minute! If the neighbor goes on a diet or gets diarrhea, why feed us the same food, woman?" She shuts me up by saying, "Well *they* eat it; don't they count?" "Madam, have our stomachs become the same as theirs? Drop these people. Let's look after our own lives!" I say, but they never listen!

If it were just my wife, to a certain degree I'd be quiet and pull in my horns, but the children are just like their mother. Last night the older girl said, "Please, Daddy, I have to have crutches." "But, daughter what will you do with crutches? You're not lame, thank God!" The girl looked me in the eye and replied, "What if I were?" "Oh, that's easy," I said, "then we'd get you some." You don't know how insistent the girl was! Gosh, our neighbor's two girls got crutches and went around on them all day at school. Their friends flocked around in concern and curiosity. They loved the big show the girls were putting on. They were pulling a big deal at school. When their teachers asked them why the crutches, they said they were going to take skiing lessons this winter. They were learning to walk with crutches ahead of time to prepare for any accident that might happen. What a stupid excuse! Good grief! Could you swallow this baloney? We did. We swallowed it hook, line, and sinker. We went and bought the three children crutches. Before the week was out, the whole neighborhood was filled with children on crutches. Dumb little bastards, not one of you is lame; where did this fad come from? Oh, the poor ruined fathers! They don't control their daughters, the daughters control them! Two houses below us, there's an Egyptian family. The man was originally an Armenian from Istanbul. Last night I cornered him. "My God, what's happening to us? These damn kids aren't lame, there's nothing wrong with them. Why do we buy these crutches for them? It's disgraceful, isn't it?"

Discontent

"Friend, I don't humiliate my own children," he said. "They just asked for them once; should I say no? Might as well buy them! Why not? Don't be old-fashioned, monsieur! It's not right to leave them ignorant because they're girls. Teach them whatever you can! It's all useful."

I saw that it just wasn't going to work out, so we moved out of the neighborhood. We bought a home in a quiet area on the south side of town. Thank God, my business was thriving. Our butcher shop was busy as a beehive. Money was flowing like water in the Seyhan River. We bought new furniture for the house and a big automobile. At my wife's request, we bought brand-new clothes for everybody before we moved to the new house. We hired a gardener and a cook. Oh, finally, I was happy with my life. "This is it!" I exulted. We were saved from our neighbors' troubles! My wife, binoculars in hand, would no longer spy on them! She would no longer watch everything they did. The children wouldn't demand that we buy just anything. Comfort at last, friend!

Our new neighborhood was nice. Charming houses with red, green, or yellow tile roofs under the shadows of giant trees. Those living on our street were all wealthy, cultured people. No one paid any attention to anyone else. They didn't even know each other's names. Oh, what a sweet life! Thank God we found ourselves a nice place. My wife and children found their old pleasures. No longer did they ask what someone wore, ate, or bought. Everyone interested himself in his own life.

But this dream of ours lasted but a short while. One night, when I came home, I couldn't find anyone. I heard sounds from downstairs. I went down and looked. My eldest daughter was sobbing. When I asked, "Hello, daughter, what's the matter?" she opened her mouth and closed her eyes. Oh, what a bad father I was! "You're making Mother miserable!" she cried. That day, my wife had gone to a doctor who told her she should go on a trip to some warm place and rest. If she continued as she was, wan and pale, she would get sick.

"Very well, where is your mother now?" I asked. "Lying down upstairs," she replied. I went up and checked. My wife was lying stretched out as if she were half dead. "See what you've done to

Discontent

me, sir! I'm dead, finished! My doctor told me that if I don't go to some sunny place, I'll soon die! Oh, what have I done to deserve this? And if you don't believe me, watch the television. All the film stars this year have gone to Florida and California to take advantage of the sun. They're all brown as Arabs. The best doctors in the world recommend the beach for health."

We borrowed here and there and decided to take everyone in the family to Miami. The shopping to buy necessities for the trip lasted a week. Seven night garments, fifteen new bathing suits, ten pairs of shoes, a flock of underwear. That day, as if they'd promised each other, the whole street was on the plane. Everyone was going to Miami. Damn, where did these home wreckers come from? And I had thought we were safe from this trouble. The whole neighborhood was off to tan their skins! Even the black doctor who just moved to our street was there!

We stayed at the beach for three weeks. It really was a splendid place. We returned home thoroughly tanned. We had had a good time with our neighbors there. We became quite chummy with everyone. The Mrs. took over. When she started to talk, she didn't know when to stop. She name-dropped and put on airs about our life in Turkey. It was all news to me. We had lots of automobiles at our door, chauffeurs, cooks, gardeners! Trips to Europe every year! If we had all that, why in hell did we come here? She had a ready answer for that, too. Well, sir, butchering in our country is primitive, so we came here to learn the business. Have you ever heard such bull? Yet in a way I kind of liked it. "Even if it's a lie, go ahead and tell them, lady!" I said to myself. After returning from Miami, everyone set up a telescope and aimed it at our house. If we ate beans, everyone ate beans! I beg your pardon, if we made out, they made out too, all together, in a chorus!

The last incident exhausted my patience. Last week we went and bought a new television. It was a magnificent instrument, the latest model. It projected pictures on the wall. We viewed it like the movies. Before the week was out, the whole neighborhood was filled with the same model. Even the blind, retired colonel on the corner bought one. "OK!" he said, "even if I can't see it, I listen to the music now and then!"

Discontent

Yesterday, I kissed my wife on the cheek for the last time. We had decided to separate as friends. It had been a whole twenty-five years since we married. According to the rules around here, children of couples who remain married to the same mate will raise their own children poorly. After twenty-five years of marriage we were separating. How could we tell the children? Would we be able to handle this business without offending or saddening them? I tried to organize in my mind how I would break it to them. Finally, I decided to tell it the way it was. I faced my son and daughter and started to explain. Both of them had sweet smiles on their faces. They were so unworldly! They sat and looked at me with no idea of what was about to happen to them.

While I was explaining, the boy interrupted. "Dad," he said, "congratulations! We were unhappy because we saw you were so old-fashioned. We were saying, 'How did God give us such ignorant parents?' Thank the Lord, you noticed. We've been hoping for this for a long time. Kids our age have had two or three fathers or mothers already. You should see such happy children! Every new father buys a flock of presents for his new children. Now you're straightened out. Actually, I'm thinking of my little brother. I was worried about his growing up in an environment so lacking in culture. Because of you, we were always ashamed at school!"

Before the month was out, the neighborhood scattered like a covey of quail. Divorce, divorce! They all sneaked away somewhere! That's how it is. Now I forget about being in my fifties and chase young things twenty-five years old. Really, it's almost futile at this age, but what can you do, it's a matter of habit!"

CHINESE TUEY

Chinese Tuey, with slight wispy body and large head, blew in the wind. He was soft and slipped through your fingers like water. He couldn't stay on top of a hill, but quickly slid down it. In the street, whether windy or not, he waved like a flag and, recently, it seemed impossible to have a proper word or two with Tuey. He either flew off like a balloon in the wind or flowed to the bottom of the hill like water. To hold him long enough to complete your sentence, you would either have to hammer him into the ground by his feet like a stake or tie him to a tree.

The muscles of Tuey's face were pulled tight, as if in a perpetual smile, which looked good on him. His Chinese face had a yellow complexion and white teeth but his eyes were bloodshot like the meat of an Istanbul melon; in his rumpled clothes, he resembled a squashed apricot.

One noon I chanced across Tuey in the Chinese Market park, that little park surrounded by giant buildings, in the heart of Montreal. Among those skyscrapers, the city had made a park of the tiny open space which the sun licked between one and two-thirty in the afternoon. Children of Chinese families living in the heart of the city came to this park six months out of the year to learn about the sweet warm rays of the sun. In this part of the city, the sunlight was sought only when necessary, like penicillin or aspirin. Perhaps the leader of the community didn't care much for sunshine. Why should he? From many points of view, the sunlight was harmful to people who carried on their lives here. First of all, sunlight hurt one's eyes. Just as people coming out of a dark movie have their eyes so bedazzled they can't see in the light, Chinese from the heart of the city, when they got a chance to visit the country and mountains, found their eyes and hearts were so dazed they couldn't see anything either.

The Chinese had become shy and timid, like mice who live in secluded places. Unused to sunshine and fresh air, they became confused when face to face with nature; some stood petrified with fear while others shouted songs as loudly as they could. The Chinese Market was full of children who had never seen a bird, cow, horse, donkey, or bee.

If one considers what happened to Tuey, the young Chinese should have died off in the streets long ago. But they obstinately lived on. With the stubbornness of goats, they carried on their lives.

Without bothering to say, "How do you do?" Tuey began telling his story:

May God not confuse anyone! Once, we were confused! Our comfort and tranquility were disturbed! Thank heaven, my store is very small, but it makes good money. We lack for nothing. We decided to move from this dark, sunless, airless place. Spring breezes had begun blowing in my wife's mind! Like this crazy world, we too started spinning in space! See that skyscraper over there, that building which has one end buried in the earth and the other end in the clouds? We rented a one-bedroom flat on the thirty-seventh floor of that high-rise. People had said, "The view is beautiful!" We went up and looked. Truly, the whole city was spread out under our feet like a carpet. In the center of the pearl-strewn city, like a black belt, stretched a dark river. I couldn't get enough of looking at it in the moonlight.

You should view this dirty world you see here from the thirty-seventh floor! A thousand witnesses couldn't make you believe it's the same city! The air you breathe into your lungs there is entirely different—clean and pure! It smells of cologne, pine, juniper—as soft as a cloud. Friend, we put out the five hundred dollars a month and moved to our home in the sky. The first night, in our excitement, we couldn't sleep. All night we sat and talked about the beautiful view. The next day, I closed the shop early. The sleep in my eyes felt like five pounds of honey! Oh-h-h, I thought, I'll trot on home and stretch out there!

I no sooner stretched out than my wife said, "Please, Honorable Tuey, are we spending five hundred dollars a month to sleep? We can sleep anytime. Look, everyone pays money and flies in planes to see the world. They go to Europe. Now come and look at this magnificent city!"

Truly, it was a divine world below! A torchlight parade appeared, like an army of soldiers; two fires were burning on the east side of town. In the dusty, pale blue city darkness, the flames glowed like oranges. Enthusiastically, we watched the fires from the thirty-seventh floor.

We saw the sunrise in the dawn. I saw the sun that large for the first time. On the third day, due to fatigue, sleeplessness, and hunger, I turned into a corpse. Soon, I would be picked up by the city police for leaving a body in the streets without permission.

On the following nights, we viewed the south, north, river, mountains, stars, clouds, distance, silence, and solitude. We waited for more fires, which would have entertained us even more, but no one's house burned.

Eight days, I worked in my shop, eight nights, I longed for the fairy-tale city. At the end of the eighth, I had lost fifty pounds. I could no longer stand on my feet. Before dying, I just wanted to sleep my fill. Not one corner of the city was left for me to view. From the thirty-seventh floor, like the saints, we had perceived the filthy, dirty, sick world as bright and magnificent.

On the ninth night, just as I had determined to go to bed early, someone knocked. Our friends, the Hueys, and their children had come to visit. On the tenth night, the Tangs, Yus, Sin-sus, their daughter-in-law and grandchildren, the Hans, distant kinsmen, and their neighbors had come to see the city. On the eleventh night, the Yengs, two daughters, their fathers-in-law, their uncles, recently arrived from Hong Kong with their three children, and again the Yengs' old neighbors, Groceryman Ti, and all our Chinese neighbors on the whole street came to honor our home.

We clenched our teeth! "Somehow this rush will end one day!" we said. It didn't end! On the contrary it got wilder! They started coming in the daytime, too. Chinese Priest Chung, who was trying to teach his students at the church about the rivers, mountains, forests, birds, field mice, squirrels, silence, cleanliness, clouds, and sun and how they affected society, wanted permission from us to bring them in turn to our apartment. Could you say, "Come! You're welcome!" if it were you?

CHICKEN THIEF

That day before sunrise, the people of Kagnawaga Village awakened to a frightful row. Before dawn, before the river down the slope was visible, the old Indian, Windfoot, was yelling his head off, cussing like mad. Windfoot had awakened the whole village. He was mad! Beating together two empty gas cans he'd gotten hold of, he shook up the whole village. All its inhabitants laughed and said, "That crazy redskin has the whole place at loggerheads again!" Windfoot kept banging the cans savagely and yelling murderously.

The Indian was an arrogant, obstinate fellow. In his little shack, which was about to collapse on the bank of the river, he carried on his life, aloof from everyone. He fished from the shore from morning till night. He never went to church, drank beer, got drunk, or talked with anyone. His face was a mass of wrinkles, as if, in order to create that face, God had used at least three times the skin He used for any other person's face. There were wrinkles on wrinkles. No one knew how old Windfoot was and no one liked him. However, because he harmed no one, they tolerated his orneriness.

His relations with the priest were bad, too. Quite some time back, when the priest first tried to help Windfoot, the Indian angrily snapped at him. Since then, whenever he comes to Windfoot's assistance, he always gets snapped at. All the villagers are angry with the Indian. Did this good-for-nothing old fellow think he was a better man than they? The kindly priest reached out his hand to help everyone; he helped everybody as much as he could. Everyone else happily accepted the priest's compassion. Only this stiff-necked fellow turned his back. No matter how many times the priest took him medicine or food, Windfoot poured them on the ground right in front of his eyes.

Chicken Thief

Recently, unprecedented things had happened to the old Indian. This wasn't the first theft in the village. For some time these outrages had been going on. The first incident began this way: On a beautiful summer morning, Kagnawaga Village awakened to an uproar. The villagers all thought that Deccal, the evil spirit of doomsday, had descended upon them. Frightened out of their wits, they ran about like children. Earth and sky reverberated, "Boom, boom!" The villagers ran out of their houses. The old Indian, half naked, wearing pants only, with an empty can in each hand, was doing a rain dance in the village square while singing an incomprehensible song.

He looked at no one. Shouting, "Hey-ya, Hey-ya!" he banged the cans together and, spinning on one foot, kept on yammering. The village elders tried to calm the crazy old man. But he listened to nobody and, holding to the strange rhythm, turned like a pinwheel, singing, "Hey-ya, Hey-ya, I want my chicken!" At this point the village priest arrived. "Windfoot!" he said, "Did someone steal your chicken? Here's three dollars for you; go buy yourself two chickens with this money!" He was afraid that the Indian would throw it on the ground. But Windfoot snatched the money and ran to his shack. That noon, the priest took the old man a bowl of chicken soup and bread. Everyone was surprised because he accepted help from the priest for the first time.

The good-hearted priest was happy. His help had finally touched the forlorn old Indian. Talk about the chicken thieving continued for a few days, then finally subsided. This was the first thievery in the village when the culprit wasn't caught.

Before three or four days had passed, again the villagers were awakened by an uproar. This time it seemed the noise was coming from all directions at once. Ten crazy warriors, in ten different places, were beating drums. The villagers rushed outside. The old Indian had tied three gas cans to one of the limbs on each of ten trees, connected them with rope, then sat on a rock where he was yanking the rope and yelling his head off. "Hey-ya, Hey-ya! I want my chickens, I want my chickens!" This time, two of the old man's chickens had been stolen. All the villagers, still in their nightclothes, went searching for the old man's chickens in the early-morning dark-

Chicken Thief

ness. They looked in every coop, every nook and corner. Lighting torches, they searched homes and stables. It seemed as if the earth had opened up and swallowed the chickens. The villagers knew they wouldn't get a wink of sleep before the chickens were found.

When they returned and said they couldn't find anything, old Windfoot pulled harder on the rope, filling the sky with unendurable clamor. Nowhere could one escape from it. "Please, we beg of you!" implored the villagers. "Stop this racket, Windfoot! You've ruined our sleep! You woke up all the babies, all the old folks in the village, and made them miserable! Come on, don't keep this up until morning. When it's daylight, we'll find your lousy chickens." But Windfoot wasn't about to listen to anyone.

Once more, it fell to the lot of our good priest to save the village from disaster. He pressed six dollars into the Indian's hand. Windfoot's eyes gleamed when he saw the money. He snatched it and ran off to his shack. All the villagers admired the priest. Again, he had saved both the village and the old man from trouble. Later, the priest presented him with chicken soup and meat so he wouldn't be hungry for a couple of days.

Windfoot's obstinacy continued. In spite of all the priest's assistance, the old Indian hadn't thanked him once. The villagers said, "Never has anyone returned kindness with such rudeness!"

No sooner had the incident been forgotten and the Indian lapsed into his old contrary ways than a new theft would again turn the place into confusion and anarchy. Each time the priest would come to the village's rescue and calm things down.

The villagers slowly became accustomed to these goings-on. In fact, they even enjoyed them. No one could find out who the sly thief was. Of course, everyone had something to say about it. Some said teenagers could have done it and others claimed it was the crazy Indian who did away with the chickens himself. Yet nobody knew the truth of the matter. These thefts had become an entertainment for the people. Each time, Windfoot found some new way to rouse the village.

Then the latest theft occurred: Kagnawaga Village was again awakened by a hubbub. aughing, the villagers came out of their houses and waited in curiosity to see how that day's entertainment

Chicken Thief

would go. The crazy old man was banging cans together and singing his strange song, "Come see! I caught the thief!" he sang. All ran to Windfoot's house. The priest was tied to a great tree on the bank of the river.

The old Indian stood in front of the priest and looked him in the eye. Then, beating cans together, he sang his song and, hopping his one-legged dance, whirled around the tree. All the people of the village stared at him in disbelief. "Here's the low-down thief!" he shouted, "Hey-ya, Hey-ya! All night I waited for the thief. When I heard him make a noise, I fired both barrels through the chicken-coop door! I killed all the chickens, but I winged the thief, too!" Then Windfoot cut the rope and released the priest. Without looking back, he ran limping to the church and disappeared inside.

LIVING CHEAP

"I'm just never going to be well! I'm through, done, finished! I'm going to die and remain in this foreign land. Before I kick the bucket, I'll make peace with my friends. I won't attract anyone's attention. By the sweat of my brow, I've paid off the house. All my debts are paid, thank God! Like a young girl preparing for her wedding, I'm getting ready for the death that awaits me. There isn't a doctor in this whole big city I haven't seen. I've had myself extensively examined from head to toe. All of them said the same thing! They laughed and threw me out the door! This February, I'm completing my second year. In two years, I've been examined by no less than six hundred ten doctors. All of them know me now! As soon as I say my name, their secretaries put me off and won't give me an appointment. If I tell them my trouble, they laugh out loud. They go completely out of their way to put me off with trumped-up excuses. I'm really fed up! Most important, I'm worn out from being given the runaround. May God curse this place! This big city will be my grave! Yet, once I was living so well! My work was comfortable, the money good. I didn't spend more than I made. We had a nice happy home . . .

"Anyway, this curse of God hit after we bought color television! Family harmony flew out the window! First of all, pleasant conversation ceased. No one spoke with anyone else the livelong day. All tried to convey their troubles with hand signals. Then they headed for the TV. I held my tongue until it was numb. Just as unused arm and leg muscles do, my tongue atrophied. I couldn't drink, couldn't eat! If I opened my mouth, a flock of strange noises came out instead of understandable speech. 'Oh, God, look what's happened!' I cried, and I rushed to the doctor. With signs and writing, I told him, 'Please, doctor, measure my tongue! My tongue is shrinking!' First the doctor examined my mouth carefully. 'You have nothing wrong,' he said. When I insisted, he replied, 'Such a thing is not possible!' He sent me to a psychiatrist. You've never seen such a dishonorable wretch! He intended to diagnose me as being crazy! It's a blessing that my symptoms soon disappeared. My voice came back. Yet oh, if only I hadn't recovered! When this problem ended, a new one began. I couldn't escape from continual trouble. . . ."

The man telling this story was a Hungarian immigrant, about fifty, a short, fat man. He was sitting beside me on the commuter train and pouring out his troubles. I became interested and asked him a few questions. At home, he had two grown daughters and a son of university age. He looked sad and tired, like a man who had lost everything. "Alas," he said, "last summer I took a week off and stayed home! I didn't go anywhere. 'Let's rest a little,' I said to myself, but I regretted it the whole week long! By the weekend, I was confined to bed with a high fever. They rushed me to the hospital. Upon examination they found that the whole week long—I beg your pardon—I had forgotten to go to the toilet! God save us from watching TV! How can a person forget to go to the toilet? He just forgets! He plain forgets! Be careful, if you sit in front of that damn box the whole day, you too will start acting like a nincompoop.

"Furthermore, friend, I have a weak stomach! I can't eat just anything! I have to diet. Otherwise, God forbid, I get nauseated. It's impossible to stand the way my stomach growls. My insides explode like fireworks at the fairgrounds! Sound erupts from my mouth, nose, ears, and eyes. If we were strangers and, quite by accident, I had a belching crisis while you were beside me, you wouldn't know what had happened and might be frightened to death. Recently, at the bus stop, a woman had a miscarriage because of me! They took me to court and harassed me. I was very sorry for the woman, truly! She was standing beside me when suddenly there was a rumble, a roar; she let out a scream and . . . don't ask! From fright, she miscarried on the spot, the poor woman.

"I rushed to the doctor. After a thorough examination, he said, 'Be careful what you eat. Your stomach is sound as a dollar. It's only that you get an upset stomach after eating too much. Stay away from foods that cause gas. Eat sparingly!' he said. Well, to be truthful, the interval between my meals isn't very long. Whether I eat or not won't change things much for me. But, let's see you come and diet in front of the television. Can you do it? Is it possible for anyone?

"First, on the screen you see a turkey broiled golden brown. Beside it is a goblet of ice-cold white wine! You are beside a pool. You're neither hungry nor thirsty but slowly your mouth starts to water. This is a TV commercial for a firm that sells turkeys. You can't stand it. 'Madam, is there any turkey in the house?' you ask. My wife's voice, coming from the kitchen, says, 'Hey, didn't we just eat?' The poor woman didn't see the ad so how could she understand? She takes the turkey out of the freezer. At ten o'clock at night, she cooks it and it's eaten. Soon comes a commercial for oranges on the TV . . . they cut the orange in half and hold it out to you . . . there are a few drops of juice on it. That shows how fresh it is! Then a hand slowly squeezes the orange. Before two seconds, your mouth has watered. Yell again, 'Madam, make some orange juice and let's have a drink!'

"It's evening and let's say you're watching a cowboy film. Every ten minutes there's a commercial about food. Come on, don't eat! Can't you control yourself? First a warm tropical island and the tantalizing scent of bananas . . . nude native women carrying the yellow bananas toward a sky-blue lagoon. Then, also in full color, the Himalaya Mountains appear, shrouded in snow. They're lost in snow and ice. The camera slowly zooms in on the peak, and in icy droplets you see a bottle of 7-Up. Even if you're not thirsty, you'll drink the damn thing.

"We finally became adjusted to some things! For example, every January I gain about ten kilos. Then, to lose weight, I stay in the hospital for a week each February. Why? Very simple! Beginning in January, all the unsold cakes, sweets, and cookies left over from Christmas and New Year's are sold at half-price—to help the poor. Could you resist buying and eating all these goodies at half-price? You fill the house with them as if there's been a famine. By the time it's May, pimples erupt on my face, because they are selling last year's pickles at three-fourths off. Every May we go on a pickle binge. After that, come check us out! Our faces all blossom out with pimples like plum trees . . .

"The worst is June. I drop from seventy kilos to fifty. You see this man with the big belly? I want you to know that in June he's fallen to fifty kilos. In June, the sport commercials start on TV. All day, the announcers lecture you to lose weight. Everything you eat produces cholesterol! Don't eat meat, don't eat chicken! Don't eat this, don't eat that! Don't eat anything! The stomach shrinks and shrinks! If the wind blows, you'll fall down! Again, you rush to the doctor!

"Midsummer is still another problem. This time the vitamin regimen begins. Vitamins mornings, vitamins evenings! From swallowing so many vitamins, we itch and scratch like mangy donkeys. Again, run to the doctors!

"However, the latest ads on TV have completed my ruin. This time, I'm surely on my way out, I can't believe I'll survive! It's cancer! All the symptoms are plain as day. I have lung cancer! But those low-down doctors say, 'No!' They're deceiving me! I have all the symptoms shown on television. Therefore, after due deliberation, I'm preparing for death. If I find a grave plot cheap, I'll buy it, in advance. If a person knows, let him announce it! He should tell his wife and friends, for God's sake!"

NO ONE TO YELL AT

Kazim Aga from Kayseri was mad as a hornet. He was cursing everything from hell to breakfast. "Damn country!" he yelled. "It's not a country, it's an insane asylum! Nobody has any brains! Something goes wrong and they don't even care! These dull, cowardly dogs, by God! The bastards have no guts! Like a bunch of blockheads. No love, no enthusiasm! If their pants caught fire, they wouldn't put it out without permission from their wives, the idiots! Everything is carefully calculated. Damn such a life! Our money disgraces us. There's no pleasure or charm! Does living here have to be like this? Man, we have everything; we should live like pashas. But we've become coolies wearing ties! In Adana, even my clerk had more pleasure and fun. At least, on holidays, I gave him some spending money and sent him to a bar to enjoy himself. And he knew how to be a clerk; on occasion he came, kissed my hand, and asked after my health. Is it like that in this damn country? Just look at that old guy sitting over there! Has anyone ever seen him grin? Not on your life!

"I go to the bank and deposit wads of money; I withdraw money. Does that insensitive fool, that so-called director, ever offer me tea or coffee, or even a Coke? Never, never!"

In Old Montreal, on a street below the great Notre Dame Cathedral, stands the business place belonging to our Kazim Aga. He wholesales imported crystal giftware from Eastern-European countries. His business seems to go well, but whenever I go to see him, he complains about his situation. Sometimes he plays backgammon with his Lebanese neighbor, a carpet man. When he loses, he's mad at losing, and when he wins, he's mad because he can't make a rural Arab angry. "I can't get a fellah mad," he complains, swallowing his anger.

No One to Yell At

It was as if the city were on fire that last week in June. The sun blazed in the sky. Narrow streets were filled with idly wandering tourists and young secretaries from neighboring banks. From time to time, the sound of steamships came from the harbor. This area is back of Old Montreal's harbor. The buildings are old and dirty, their walls thick. Wholesalers have occupied this part of the city from way back. However, now, with help from the Montreal city government, a restaurant has been opened on every corner.

A phaeton was parked at the door. It was a one-horse, pretty coach with a fold-down top. Kazim Aga rushed to the window to look at the vehicle. "I love that coach. When I look at it I'm cheered up. If I could, I'd ride it to and from home every day. But it's expensive! The guy drove me once and took me for fifteen dollars. I swore never to ride it again."

When I came in, Kazim Aga had stopped his yelling. I go to visit him during noon-hour from time to time. He's a pleasant man, easy to talk with. Though he appears ignorant, he's really a sharp country boy with lots of common sense. When it comes to money business, or people, he rarely makes a mistake.

Upon seeing me, he said, "Come in and have a coffee. There's something I want to tell you." He sent one of the employees working beside him, to the nearby coffee man to get two Turkish coffees. The young woman left with a sour look on her face.

"Did you see that hussy?" he said, "I pay these people lots of money but they don't want to take two steps to fetch a cup of coffee. That slip of a girl complained to the accountant about me. 'I'm no coffee girl,' she said. 'If he's going to send me for coffee all the time I won't work here.' I told the accountant, 'You tell that girl that I'll not only send her, but the accountant himself if I want to.' Nonsense! If we take jobs, we all must work. If I want, I'll even have her sweep the shop. But, after all, I don't want to judge the young woman. You see all these sons-of-bitches! Spend a wad of money on them, give them jobs, and they all defy you. We couldn't find even one good Moslem to hire. This is the third girl we've tried. Women don't stay long. And I pay them plenty, too! I don't cut their pay the way those other Greek Turks do. Shall I tell you something, sir? Life here doesn't suit me! It's empty, cheerless! As my father used to say, 'Life has to have some charm and pleasure!'

"In Adana, I had a little store with a clerk and errand boy. I used to send my errand boy, little Kürt Hasso, to the market to get food and vegetables for the house. Every evening, he swept the store, too. You know, those two were the charm of my life. Sir, we worked together all those years and I didn't offend them even once. We got along together like a big family. They knew how to be errand boy and clerk and I knew how to be boss. On holidays, they came to kiss my hand and I never failed to open my wallet and pay them a bonus. With that life, they were happy, I was happy! When things went wrong, at least I had someone to yell at and curse. If I was upset, I swore at Hasso; I yelled at Hasso. And he would say, 'Good health to you, boss, get mad at me rather than a stranger,' and pacify me, the son-of-a-bitch. I swore at Hasso over little things. If big things went wrong, and I needed someone bigger to curse, I yelled at the clerk, Emin Effendi. He didn't usually answer. He didn't say 'thank you' or 'to your good health.' Perhaps the man hid his anger. Anyway, he never forgot his gentlemanly behavior; he knew his place and, if unwillingly, accepted the cursing with good manners. Never, at any time, did either of them abandon his gentlemanly behavior because I got mad and cursed them. Neither ever stopped me or gave me a cross answer. Being a well-bred man is really something, my friend! Look at the dirty fellows around here! Do they have even a trace of courtesy? Doesn't it ever occur to them to say, 'This is the boss, the owner; naturally he swears, he has a right to.' No one says, 'Let's be a little help to a man who takes all these troubles on his shoulders. Let's tolerate the poor guy's being all upset.' These infidels are ungrateful, by God! They jabber away, but I never listen! I swear the way I know how, in Turkish! But I don't get the same flavor out of it, because they don't understand.

"You know what I decided to do? I've decided to bring Hasso over here. Yesterday, I sat down and wrote him a letter and invited him. 'Come!' I said, 'I'll give you a good monthly salary, bed and board is on me, and I'll pay your doctor bills. I'll pay for your clothes, too.' I told Hasso, 'It's your day again, Hasso. You son-of-a-bitch, come over and see a little country!'

"I'm truly pleased that Hasso is coming. I'll have someone around to curse and yell at. At least, when I swear, the guy has to know, to understand what I say. He mustn't just stare at me stupidly. As far as I'm concerned, Hasso is used to swearing. He couldn't stand not being sworn at. One time, I didn't curse Hasso for a whole week. Whether I was very busy or sick I can't remember. Anyway, I hadn't found a chance to yell for a week. You'll like what Hasso told me that weekend: 'Boss, it's clear you are sick! You haven't opened your mouth and said anything all week. You haven't sworn! Swear, swear and relax, boss, don't stay upset like that!' Have you ever seen such an intelligent man? He can ask me for anything he wants; I'd give my life to one like that. But, he must always know his place...."

STRIKES

Free countries accept strikes as natural. Especially in the years following rapid inflation, strikes become daily and commonplace events. On days when there are no strikes, things go wrong, people become confused, in short they're reduced to clumsiness. The strikes that have broken out in Montreal the past year demonstrate this.

Mondays the bus drivers strike. Tuesdays the firemen, Wednesdays the doctors, Thursdays the elevator repairmen, nurses, and gravediggers. Fridays the strikes of the newspaper and restaurant workers, ground forces units, and airline employees take place, and Saturday those of the optometrists, pharmacy workers, priests, sextons, paper factories, and railroad workers. The only day left for the police to strike was Sunday. They humbled themselves and accepted that day when as a matter of fact they would have preferred Tuesday. They couldn't strike then because the firemen, who were more pushy, snatched Tuesday up for themselves.

Until we got used to this social phenomenon, we suffered numerous difficulties. However, finally we adjusted to the situation fairly well. Now, we even like it. It adds color and excitement to our lives. We are not strong supporters of those who would change it. Where would we find a better life than this? Just let me tell you about it.

Mondays I stay home because there's no bus to ride to work. Now, staying home doesn't mean that I just laze around! On Mondays, I cook all day. Why? Very Simple! As the firemen are on strike Tuesday, we have no fires at home that day. Why do we need one? You have to be careful with fire! How could you extinguish a fire? It's better to stay awake than have a nightmare; better safe than sorry! So Tuesdays we rest and unload all our fatigue.

Strikes

On Tuesdays, we also take special care with our food. We look after our health because on Wednesdays the doctors are on strike. One eats one's food carefully, drives safely, and takes unusual measures to make sure the children don't fall and injure their heads. No one throws apple or banana peels on the sidewalks. Out-of-doors, everyone walks cautiously. I haven't yet encountered anyone who ran or hurried. If anyone did, it would have to be a tourist from the States.

Thursdays are days of rest for employees working on floors higher than the eleventh. Those working above the eleventh floor aren't brave enough to go higher because the elevator repairmen are on strike and they're afraid the elevator will break down when there's no one to fix it. That day it's almost impossible to find room on the elevator as far as the eleventh floor. Officials and lady secretaries living in high-rise apartments don't go home but reserve rooms in hotels. It's hard to follow the Thursday program. The nurses and gravediggers being on strike, such difficult-to-control events as sickness and death can cause a lot of trouble. So if you're thinking about it Thursdays, don't get sick, don't die! Really, the strikers don't give a damn about anybody! You'll be left crawling in the streets! On Fridays, there not being local or world news, our lives pass sweetly and happily. That day no one fights with anyone. No one busts anyone in the face. You can't imagine how restful it is with the newspapers closed. It being Friday, the politicians are wrapped in a profound silence. They can't put forth even the tiniest pearl of wisdom before Saturday. In this period, Friday, all the workers go on a strict diet. As a special result of the restaurants being closed, Canadians have been prevented from becoming obese.

Who said communist Russia was an evil country? On the contrary, we're very happy with Russia. What Russia has done for us, a father wouldn't do for his son. Why not? Due to the ground force units going on strike Saturdays, our Minister of State has requested Russia not to attack on Saturdays and the Russians have accepted our proposal. When it's Saturday, the city is wrapped in a delightful silence. Priests also being on strike, city church bells allow pigeons and people who are not deaf to take a deep breath.

Strikes

As for Sunday, no one leaves the house. They're afraid to leave and go anywhere because of insecurity due to the police being on strike. One of the daily events here is for a large house to be lifted off its foundations, loaded on a long truck, and moved to another location all in a couple of hours. Some houses are made in factories and moved by truck to the lot where they'll be located. People who live in these won't go anywhere on days when the police are on strike. It's common to find an empty lot in place of a house upon returning home. Now, when I see a great house being carried on a truck, I laugh to myself, saying, "I wonder whose house they're taking away this time."

COMPUTERS

Our every activity depends on the computer and the statistics it spews out. Our lives, travel, entertainment, our deaths—in summary, everything we have is tied to it. It's as if, like puppets controlled with strings, we are all tied to the computer. If you're going to get married, it chooses the best mate. If you want to become rich, to live a healthy life, ask it; the answer is ready. Your name? Age? Occupation? Spouse? I beg your pardon, how many times a week do you do it with your wife? Please excuse this inappropriate question, but I have to ask it too: Do you have regular bowel movements? What month and where were you born? What foods do you like? What do you eat the most of daily? Do you drive an automobile? How many thousand miles per year do you drive? Do you covet your neighbor's wife? Do you often travel to foreign countries?

Now, if you answer all these questions truthfully, the computer will inform you to what age you will live and where and of what you will die. The answer it gives will be ninety-nine point nine percent correct. There's no escape, my friend!

This has to be what the ancients referred to as "the Grim Reaper"! If he places his hand on your shoulder and says, "You died!" just don't try to keep on living. If you have any sense, you'll stretch out on the ground right where you are and close your eyes. Once that machine says, "He died!" your name is removed from the population register. It cancels your hospital and doctor cards. If you have no card, just try to see a doctor! If you die in the street they won't even turn to glance your way! It cancels your unemployment insurance. Try to find a job, if you're a man; you won't have a chance! This computer is an amazingly good thing but, thank God, these

Computers

things I've mentioned don't really happen because when the machine decides you're dead, believe me, you *are* dead!

The computer has entered every step of our lives. It pays our salaries, it pays our taxes, it registers debits in our bank accounts. It announces when we'll have accidents, directs traffic, prepares weekly weather forecasts, and foretells economic developments, unemployment increases, and inflation decreases. For example, let me explain this week's situation. Sunday we're closed. According to the computer, this week there will be twenty-seven automobile accidents, fifty-seven people will die, and there will be three drowning accidents, seven fires, three rapes, and two family fights. If you wish, let's take a look at the coming Tuesday. You will see that it conforms perfectly! The machine publishes before your eyes as statistical fact the weather, precipitation, population increase, profit situation, beverage sales increases, dissatisfaction of people with their lives, their neglect, husband and wife fights, and, if it's summer, the number of girls on the streets in miniskirts, if winter, the ice conditions.

If this experience that I'm about to relate hadn't happened to me, I could have been happy with my life, happy with computers, and able to carry on my work. But it wasn't like that at all. I suffered terrible hardship.

Well, sir, when the economic situation started to go bad two months ago, the computer flashed the danger signal to all the big corporations. It informed them that in order for the market prices to fall, it was necessary to reduce the number of employees. This was an unheard-of idea! Would prices fall with two or three unfortunate employees being fired? Really a nonsensical thing! If I eat two kilos less meat and don't buy butter, eggs, and milk, would the prices of these products fall? Tell me another one! Anyway, I didn't really mind. For twenty years I had worked for a low salary at the same bank. I consoled myself, saying, "If they throw anyone out it'll be those big shots that make lots of money!"

Last month when the inflation rate reached ten percent, in order to reduce buying strength, the bank where I work sacked ten percent of its employees. That Monday, I found an envelope on my desk marked "Personal." Briefly, they thanked me and informed me that my services were terminated. Have you ever seen such a situation? I was flabbergasted! I had seven orphans at home, two dogs, a cat and also a wife! Why shouldn't I call the children of a dead man like me orphans—what name would fit them better? So I moan and groan! If I ignore it, my family will be devastated! I can't sit alone like an owl and think it over! "Damn it all, Recep!" I said to myself. Anyway, we have unemployment insurance. Even though we can hardly make ends meet, we'll probably get along somehow.

At the first of the month I went to the branch bank to close my account. I saw that money equal to my entire salary had been deposited to my account. The teller said, "This is your monthly salary." "Friend, I've been laid off! This money is not mine! Take it out of the account!" I replied. "We don't interfere with this," he said. "The computer pays your salary and now you have to take this money."

The next day I went to the General Directorate of the bank to research the situation. Thinking, "Perhaps I haven't been fired, so what's the need for all my anxiety?" I was secretly pleased. But at the General Directorate I learned that I had definitely been fired. The employee responsible for payroll said that he would straighten this business out.

At the end of the second month, to make sure that there wouldn't be trouble of any kind because I didn't take my pay, the branch informed the police. A week later, the police turned up at my door. Courteously, they invited me to the station and asked me why I didn't draw my salary; they wanted to know what I was living on. Upon hearing that I was getting unemployment insurance, they became angry. It was against the law to get unemployment insurance while drawing a salary. Furthermore, while it was right not to pay my federal taxes if I didn't draw my salary, they made it clear that I was considered a tax-evader. They explained that I was obligated to accept the money.

"I can't accept it!" I replied. "I am a man who is out of work. This money doesn't belong to me! If I take it, how will I repay it?" At police headquarters, they gave me one week to draw my pay from the bank and said that if in that period I didn't draw it, they would take me to court for tax evasion.

The next day, I tried again at the General Directorate. "Please, friends, take me back on the job and put an end to this problem! Otherwise I'll be convicted of tax evasion," I said. "Impossible!" they replied. "Once we've laid you off, we can't rehire you! But as a favor to you, we'll correct your entry in the computer."

Tired and weak, I returned home. One week, two weeks more passed. No one looked or asked for me. Oh, Mother, perhaps it's all straightened out! The police didn't bother me. At last, they weren't saying I had to draw out the money or correct the mistake. I was happy with life those days. At the end of the month, they sent my wife a widow's pension and added an orphan's allowance for the children. I couldn't understand what the damn widow and orphan pay was. I'm healthy as a radish! I wasn't dead or anything!

I told my wife, "This has to be a mistake. Give me those checks so I can go find out about this."

"No!" my wife answered. "It's not that big a mistake! This widow's pension is much more than the salary you made when you were alive. That's why I'm not very anxious to give it back."

"What are you saying, woman? Come on, am I dead? What right have you to accept government money?"

"What are you, huh? You consider yourself alive?" she retorted.

The argument with my wife lasted a week. I simply couldn't change her mind. She didn't want to lose the widow's pension she had hold of.

Finally I said, "Lord, do what you want!" I tore outside and slammed the door. Before a week had passed, my wife threw me out of the bedroom. "I don't sleep with the dead," she said. The next day we got a letter from the city. It was addressed to my wife. In the letter they informed her, "Your husband's grave is ready. If you don't bury him immediately, in conformance with appropriate ordinances, a fine of fifty dollars a day will be assessed." Our good woman became agitated and started to beg, "Please, Recep, don't ruin our family! Look, after years we finally have a sweet income; let's not destroy it because of your stubbornness. Come, let's put you in your grave before something spoils the picture. Otherwise this fine will deprive us all. It will destroy our family."

"Impossible!" I said, "Tell me, now, do I have nine lives like a cat? How can I go to my grave for no reason?"

This time my children flocked around me. "You're a traitorous father!" they said. Evidently I don't ever consider my children. Soon I'll even deprive them of a single crust of bread. After all, what's wrong with my being buried if I get out again after a couple of hours? Right while this was being argued, my wife said, "I've decided to get married, Recep! These poor children can't grow up like this. An inconsiderate husband like you would be harmful for the children. You think of no one but yourself. You don't care whether or not we're hungry and naked. You cheated the government, you recorded yourself dead! From now on you won't have to pay taxes or take a job. You'll live on air! You'll lie on your side and have a good time. I consider even one marriage with you too much. I've stood all this trouble from you! If you're not sorry about anything else, be sorry for my youth. While you were alive, we lived poorly, but just give your permission and I'll be well off now!" Would you believe it?

Anyway, although I told her, "Woman, I'm not dead, I'm still alive!" I couldn't make her listen. On the one hand, the government is looking for my corpse in order to bury me; on the other, the creditors are trying to prove me alive in order to collect their money. My wife claims I'm dead in order to get married again. Yet, the bank wants to prove I'm alive in order not to pay my pension.

As for me, I've started defending my being dead at tax time and being alive the rest of the year.

Finally, I found deliverance in escape from Canada. I have withdrawn to the untouched jungles of South America where computers have not yet penetrated. *You* should be this comfortable....

UNREGULATED CHICKEN BUTTS

I was soon to be called! I've never held a weapon in my life. My knowledge of guns doesn't go beyond six-shooters in cowboy films. If I tell you I don't know which end of a pistol to hold and which end the bullet comes out, believe me! I didn't leave the house for two days because they were going to draft me into the army. For two days I sat at the window and watched the door. I still don't know how they call a man into the army around here in Canada. Do they write him a scary letter or send a couple of officers wearing bandoliers of cartridges to pack him off to the induction center? I'm in the dark about this. I was pale, weak in the knees. At every knock on the door, I bounced up like a rubber ball. May God never let it happen to anyone! Fear is a terrible thing! You neither taste what you eat, nor know what you say. At breakfast, only after the children corrected me was I aware that I had eaten tomatoes with jam spread on them. Instead of saying "My condolences" to a Canadian friend whose mother-in-law had died, I realized only after seeing the expression on his face that I had said, "Congratulations."

Worst of all, no one was aware of the black crows floating over my head! No one saw the great danger! Friends were busy with their own lives. I sounded out a couple of people, but neither of them knew anything. If I said, "Awake, Nation, there's a war!" they'd laugh at me! Soon the American armies would wipe Canada out. Before long, the ugly American flag would wave over Montreal, Winnipeg, and Vancouver. OK, we don't say a word about our economy being run by American money, but, friend, we can't endure the American flag.

All hell broke loose because Canadian chickens, cooperating by word of mouth, laid too many eggs. More truthfully, cooperating with their butts, the chickens flooded us with eggs! As if they had nothing else to do during the long winter nights, the damn chickens laid eggs in pairs for fun. The shrewd Canadian farmers increased the proportion of calcium in the feed, turned on the lights in the spacious modern coops at midnight, and fooled the stupid chickens into thinking morning had come. Taken in by this trick, the chickens said, "Git gitgidak!" and laid their eggs. The roosters were most pleased by this activity, but, due to burnout, a number of them collapsed trying to keep the hens happy and passed away. Naturally, it's not the fate of every rooster to stand tall as a mate and start one day to double the number of his offspring. Some did survive this pleasurable task, but a number of roosters were casualties. I'll tell you about the greatest loss, however, later on.

The increased production of eggs first lowered the price. Then, we started exporting eggs to America. The first month, no sound from the Americans. President Nixon had enough troubles of his own. Why should he get involved with Canadian eggs? So the first month passed with no trouble or conflict. But the second month, the American farmer became aware of the harm cheap eggs were doing to the economy. American supermarkets were filled to overflowing with cheap Canadian eggs under the brand name of "North Star." The cheaper egg prices began to affect the sale of other foodstuffs. The sale of meat decreased four percent. Fats and sugar fell considerably. Among Americans, who eat plenty of eggs, the proportion of illnesses decreased. Unemployment appeared among doctors. In hospitals, the number of empty beds increased. A great drop in the sale of tonics and vitamins was registered. Here I must mention a rumor that in the voices of Americans who ate plenty of eggs, a big improvement was observed. It's up to you whether or not to take this claim seriously.

When Department of Commerce authorities informed President Nixon that unemployment, due to decreasing sales, had increased fifty percent, "the calf's tail broke off" as feared. At a Cabinet meeting, the bad economic situation was debated in every detail. It was decided that a strong note would be sent to friend and neighbor Canada. In summary, the note projected a clarification of these specific subjects:

Unregulated Chicken Butts

"Despite restrictions on free trade between the United States of America and Canada, the recent increased export of eggs is seen as harmful to the health of the poultry of both countries. Therefore, the Canadian government must stop these needless egg exports. The reasons the American government has set these restrictions are stated below: (1) The Canadian farmer's orienting of chickens by use of artificial means to deceive them into laying twice a day is harmful and contrary to our economic structure, which is bound to the principle of free trade. It has been suggested by University of Harvard professors that the laying of two eggs a day by Canadian chickens is contrary to the principles of free competition. (2) The broadening of the chicken's butts by laying more than one egg per day will shorten their life-span. No one must doubt that short-lived chickens will bring famine to our land in the near future. In experiments performed in modern American poultry laboratories, it was discovered that chickens whose butts are broadened will suffer difficulty in egg laying later on, and the eggs they drop will break. A study was made on the calcium deficiency in eggshells. A ten-percent breakage of eggs between the market and home was established. (3) It was also discovered that, due to their exertions, some days the chickens stopped producing yolks, that portion of the egg highest in nutrition. This situation will adversely affect the commercial, agricultural, and animal development in both countries.

"The American government urgently requests that the Canadian government take necessary measures to turn around this negative state of affairs. If they do not comply, the American government feels free to employ its military and industrial might to correct the situation."

This strong note threw the Canadian government into great confusion. In his speech concerning this incident, the Canadian Minister of Agriculture said more or less the following:

"In this circumstance, the United States of America, unfortunately, went beyond positive deportment. Her manner of conduct was one-sided and she closed her eyes to reality. America's one-sided claims are insupportable. The Canadian government's assertion that they can take under confirmation the egg-laying of chickens shows how one-sidedly these incidents have been reflected. How

Unregulated Chicken Butts

can we make our chickens do what we say? Evidently our friends have forgotten that, like the people who live in Canada, our chickens are free. To regulate chicken butts in a way parallel to high American profits is not compatible with twentieth-century free thought. As we haven't yet taken the bottoms of our people under the control of law and order, why should we work on chicken butts?

"President Nixon can't manage Canadian chicken bottoms using the same methods he tried on the Democratic Party at Watergate! Chicken butts are not the Democratic Party. The president must be aware of this!"

This reply, unfortunately, wasn't considered sufficient by the American government; it made them quite angry. The Secretary of Agriculture immediately announced that necessary measures would be taken. At this point, the American army massed on the Canadian border. We got by this calamity very cheap, friends! President Nixon's resignation saved us from great trouble. The new president, Ford, seems to be an intelligent man. He probably hasn't time to bother with our chickens. Friends, I hope everything comes out all right!

MODEST LIVELIHOOD

My Esteemed Brother, Ismail Yangöz
Mayor of Murgul,
Murgul, Turkey

I am writing you this letter from the Montreal jail. It would take too long to tell you now what I was thrown in for and what I do here. Furthermore, it's of no use to bother you with the story of my unjust treatment. It's too late! In addition, you are far away! There's no way you can help me. On the other hand, I can be of great help to you. How? Very simple, you handsome devil! All you have to do is ask! I hear that the gas from the Murgul Copper Works chimneys has wiped out all the vegetation in your area. The land is as barren as my grandmother. It no longer responds to the desires of warm breezes nor to the spring sunshine. Spring and summer pass without the land turning green or trees blossoming.

As a matter of fact, the copper plant went into production in 1951. Within three years, sulfur gas from the plant's chimneys brought trouble. All your forests and fruit trees dried up, died, and turned your town into a desert. Of course, all I know is what I read in the newspapers. I've never seen Murgul, nor will I in the future. If the police leave me alone, I'll very likely go someplace other than Murgul. The government, without pressure, has paid you sixty million lira to cover up this crime. Now I want to know what was done with the sixty million.

What you did, brother, was disgraceful. Would a man close his eyes to this rape and denuding of the nation? Never! Good grief, don't you have any intelligence or logic left? Aren't you concerned about the future of that beautiful town? Let me tell you! There'll

Modest Livelihood

be no more farming in your town! The villager will no longer plow the soil and awaken it like a young woman in bed! He will no longer cast his seed and see it germinate!

None of you will ever again see the warm spring winds melting the snow, swelling the green heads of wheat, and gently tossing tree limbs loaded with fruit. Never again can you witness the burgeoning of eggplant, squash, and tomatoes or see them bloom. You will never go out to the garden to pick melons and grapes under the July sun. In August, you won't be able to pluck lettuce and peppers to make salad hors d'oeuvres for a raki banquet. I thought you were above permitting such a thing to happen! You call that living? Just wait, there's an even worse side to this! Can a spring without flowers and plants be considered spring? Before many years the desires of all your young people will diminish and they won't seek each other. The number of married couples will decrease. Everyone will become barren. That's not all! When the land is without trees and plants, the wind will carry off the good soil and you will be left stark naked on bare rocks. Do you call this life? Go throw yourselves in the river! That is, if there's a river left in your vicinity.

Friend, there's no difference between this life you're living and blindness or death. The blind, like you, see neither the color of an orange nor the waving of grass. The dead know neither the flavor of cherries nor longing for a female. Oh, you poor fools! This trick pulled on you is the greatest swindle of the century. You're the "John" in this trick! Good Lord, if you wanted to be swindled like this, why did you go to foreigners? You had fellow countrymen over here so what sense was there in being cheated by strangers? If you had asked, couldn't we have sold you New York City? If you'd asked, wouldn't we have given you the Mississippi River? We could even have given you a proper price for the surrender of Murgul. When it comes to such lucrative propositions, why do you always run to strangers? No one screws his own friends. You dummies! How could you stand still for such a swindle? You've ruined the whole town! If you had accepted the money and then given each inhabitant of the town a million, I might have closed my eyes to some degree. But, regardless, you've still been bare-ass swindled. You've been stripped like a prize idiot with nothing to show for it. Into whose pocket did all that dough go? Am I stupid enough to tell you? Should I go to all that trouble for nothing?

Well, everything isn't as bad as it looks. Let's have a little straight talk! At least this dead ground provides a graveyard big enough for all of you. So, you didn't get to enjoy this world; everything will be wonderful in the next for sure! A ten-thousand-acre graveyard! Oh my God!

That hundred tons of sulfur gas you release into the air every day will ruin not only you but also the neighboring villages and towns. In ten years you won't be able to find air to breathe, water to drink, nor food to eat. Those who swindled you will sell you air breath by breath, water drop by drop, and bread bit by bit, and put you through hell. You will all die off. Rifat the gravedigger will be the only winner. When you die, what good will that sixty million do you?

Now let's come to my life-saving proposition. I'm making you this proposal because I love and respect you. If all goes well, we'll share the pie. But the first consideration is to save you!

As you know, I've been in America for the past ten years. I've worked at all kinds of jobs. Nine years ago, I finished New York University as an engineer. I worked at the country's largest research center as a scientist. I have a flock of new discoveries. I became closely interested in people and spent three years in prisons studying convicts. I hope that my new discoveries will be useful to you. You know that there is every kind of chemical in the human body. The foods we eat are converted into chemicals inside us. It's only logical that a way will be found to change chemicals into food. Already, I've succeeded in making bread from copper. Since copper brought you into this situation, at least you should succeed in eating it! When my new discovery goes into production, the entire town population can be fed for two months on one ton of copper. Swell deal, isn't it? Just think of the money I'll make!

My second proposal is this: I know that sulfur in some conditions is beneficial to people. Specifically, there is a close relation between sulfur and egg yolk. Using this idea, I succeeded in making yolks from sulfur. Actually, this yolk is not as tasty as chicken egg yolks, but it is edible. With this, we have solved the problem of something to eat with the bread. If you buy this discovery of mine, you will have it made for life. With the sulfur gas spewed in one day from factory chimneys, I can provide the whole town's egg requirements for a year. My research is proceeding rapidly. I believe I will succeed in making egg whites soon. After that, only the making of real eggs remains to be solved, resulting in farm eggs for the brooding hens and pullets for you. Eat, Murgul, eat!

Now, when you hear of my last discovery, your mouth will open a foot! You'll understand that your old friend hasn't spent all these years in America for nothing; I will have put the lie to our expression "a dead-end." A year ago, a friend of mine, who had sampled the air in Ankara, said, "A man who breathes Ankara air inhales poison equal to smoking ten packs of cigarettes!" I pondered these words deeply. If I could decrease the poison in the air enough, it wouldn't even be necessary for a person to smoke. I made an air filter. It filtered the air by changing the sulfur to nicotine. The results appear favorable. Just think, if I can add American cigarette flavor and taste, what great expenditures I'll save you from! With this method, I'll purify the air in the town. Due to citizens no longer smoking smuggled American cigarettes, the outflow of foreign exchange will be prevented. In summary, the most important aspect of these proposals is that while adding nutrition from sulfur to bread made of copper, you enjoy a cigarette without lighting one. It's all on me! Easy business!

Dear brother, if you're truly interested in my proposition, write me immediately at the Montreal jail.

Your brother,
Hasan Aktaş

TURK IN THE NEIGHBORHOOD

I'm just an insignificant man of fifty-three. I don't get involved with anyone. No matter what people say to me, I reply, "Yes, sir!" If they say, "Boo!" I reply, "Here, take it!" I've never been seen to get stubborn or argue with anyone. I show great care, when walking on the street, not to unnecessarily step on someone's corns. When coughing, I put my hand over my mouth, always! Summers, for fear of stepping on and crushing an ant, I never go to the country. When conversing, I never look anyone in the eye, so they won't get upset or angry at me . . . I'm a bewildered stranger here, just trying to get along. I think dogs must understand my temperament because, wherever they see me, they bark harshly at me. Then they watch me show my heels as I flee. Not only the dogs, the cats also learned this. While eating, I watched the neighbor's tabby cat snatch the meat from my plate and take off. Actually, I knew the neighbor had just fed the damned cat. It was as if the low-down feline enjoyed giving me a bad time.

It wasn't only the cats and dogs that tormented me. Everyone took advantage of my mild disposition. Our young son waylaid me recently and said, "Dad, if you don't buy me some candy, you better watch out!" Have you ever heard such rudeness? When I said, "What would you do, boy?" he replied, "Dad, I think you're good for nothing. Do you think I was just pulling your leg? You're sloppy loose with everybody else and tight with me. You give money to anyone who says, 'Boo!' yet you're stingy with your own son."

Really, what the boy said greatly distressed me. "Don't worry," I said, "I'll get you a box of candy tomorrow, my boy." He answered, "No wa-a-y! If you act like this, I'm not going to put up with it. Who cares if you buy the candy?" I was sorry for the boy, honestly. I

Turk in the Neighborhood

put on my scared act so as not to upset him. His eyes sparkled and he was pleased.

In the neighborhood, in the whole city there was no one who didn't know me. From young to old, everybody in town learned that I was a shy, mild-mannered man. Now, anyone who came along took care to scare me. I'm a man who can take a joke, but this was too much! Was there any sense in filling my hat with water or putting kittens in my pockets without provocation? I'm no small kid who enjoys all this kind of teasing. But what can you do, what else can you expect if you behave like a gentleman from Istanbul? I couldn't say anything. As much as possible I looked for ways to escape from people. I left very early in the morning and came home late at night, but still I couldn't escape them. Well, I really didn't much mind their making me angry, but those who were waylaying and scaring me on payday took my pay, which angered not only me but also my wife. After all, sir, we have a family with children; we know how to spend, too! Now just what's with this swiping our pay like that? However, no matter how I tried, I couldn't get these people to stop this amazing custom.

Finally, I found a solution by taking my wife with me to work on paydays. Even though I'm no hero, my wife is rather brave. On those days, whether it was rainy or not, she carried an umbrella and came with me. After leaving me safe and sound at work, she left. In the evening, she picked me up at work and took me home. The umbrella she carried was good for many things. In addition to using it to chase off flies, dogs, and cats, she used it as a weapon to savagely beat off the jokers who surrounded me. Thank God, with her help I found it possible to bring all my pay home.

My friends began to reproach me for going back and forth like that with my wife. Saying, "For heaven's sake! Should a person bother his wife with such trifles? She's mothering you! You're henpecked!" they tried to toy with my masculine pride. I told them, "Friends, I haven't anything to say about all these tricks you pull on me, but it's no joke when money's concerned! Because of you, my children are hungry and I listen to a lot of nagging at home! Think anything you want, brother!" and shut them up.

Turk in the Neighborhood

Later, things suddenly took on a different hue. One day at play, our small son hung the Turkish flag from the window without telling us. It was a beautiful Sunday and all the neighbors were outside.

"Heavens!" I said to my wife, "Take that flag in! There's no use bragging to the whole neighborhood that we're Turkish!" But it was too late. By the time we took the flag in, the whole neighborhood had learned who we were.

The next morning, when I went to work, my Hungarian neighbor stopped me. Yanoş lived two houses away. Whenever he'd had the chance, he had waylaid me and pulled a thousand tricks. Frankly, I was intimidated by him.

"Hello!" he said.

"Hello!" I answered.

"Are you a Turk?"

"Yes."

"Well, why didn't you say you were a Turk before? We Hungarians know Turks very well. The Turks governed us for a hundred years. Many Turkish expressions have entered our language. We have great respect for Turks. Please forgive me! Here's money for the hat I took from you as a joke and I'm giving you an extra twenty-five dollars for the trouble I caused."

He pressed a check for a hundred dollars into my hand. A little farther on, the Yugoslav, Miliç, appeared. He asked me, "Are you really Turk? I don't believe it; prove it! If you're a Turk, we've had it. I wonder if you'll forgive what we've done to you? I used to hear a lot about the Turks. Yugoslavs know the Turks very well. They governed us for one hundred fifty years. Friend, if I've wronged you, please forgive me. Last summer, my son broke two of your windows, didn't he? Here's a check for one hundred fifty dollars! It's little, but from my heart . . . For now, forgive me!" he said.

That week passed quietly in the neighborhood without incident. As soon as the children saw me from a distance, they fled. The neighbors were very respectful and shy. I encountered the Romanian, Josef, who lives on the street. When he saw me, he greeted me with a smile as if I were a friend of fifty years. Then he embraced me, saying, "Hello, my dear friend! Neighbor, I brought you a jar of *pekmez* grape syrup. I know how much Turks like *pekmez*. I used to

Turk in the Neighborhood

listen to Turkish stories when I was a boy. The Turks governed us for a hundred fifty years. Their government was much better than what we have now. At least we weren't communists. I told the Bulgarian, Alekof, that you were Turkish. You should have seen the expression on his face. You would have died laughing. 'Come on now!' he said, very embarrassed. 'I wonder if he'll forgive me?' It's clear you've suffered much harm. Friend, here's my check for a hundred fifty dollars, equivalent to your damage and loss! Here's a two-hundred-dollar check from Alekof, too. 'May he overlook what I've done!' he said. He didn't have the nerve to face you. Show your generosity and say you pardon him!"

Dear Lord, was I dreaming or something? I didn't know if what I saw was real. How quickly these neighbors, who had been mean to me and wounded my pride, changed their actions toward me. Slowly my heart filled with trust. My friends and associates had begun to understand my inner strength. My voice deepened, my stomach pains ceased, and a tone of authority appeared in my voice.

First I had to learn to get mad and yell. After all, after living for years like a slug and remaining soft, I had forgotten how. I remembered that the last time I got angry, it was at my two-year-old son. This incident had occurred ten years ago. There was no one else at home that day. When the little boy wet on me, "splash," I had become angry and said, "Ill-bred kid! But what can I expect; you're just like your mother!" I haven't lost my temper since that day. I've learned to control myself.

Money started to flow like water. The Syrian and Iraki neighbors each brought three hundred dollars and gave it to me. Thank God, no one puts me down anymore; they immediately do whatever I want.

For a time the money flow seemed cut off. I told my wife, "Take a look in that history book and see where else Turks invaded. I knew we had spread to Egypt, Lebanon, Irak, India, China, and Japan. Yet not a word has been heard from them! Have they forgotten us? Madam, why don't you visit the Egyptian family that lives on the corner? Give them a little hint that we're Turkish. Maybe they'll come to their senses and save themselves from my harsh actions." My wife replied, "Best you tell Hungarian Yanoş. He can handle it very well."

Turk in the Neighborhood

The next day, the Egyptian appeared. This Arab was pretty scared. He had a four-hundred-dollar check in his hand. "No, it won't do, friend! We don't violate anybody's rights," I said. "I'll accept only three hundred fifty dollars. We governed Egypt three hundred fifty years. Take this fifty dollars back!" He was a good person and left with a thousand prayers of gratitude.

Perhaps it would be better if I didn't tell the end of the story . . .

The next week, the Iraki, Irani, Yemeni, and North African friends came and paid their debts. Do you know who it was I couldn't wangle a dime out of? Dimitri the Greek, whom I loved the most and could never offend. Now, I won't leave him a penny in my will. Without paying a cent for all this trouble, he had flown off to Greece like a bird.

What can you do? People are all different. Some are completely honest, others a little less! Well, Dimitri was like that! Still, I hope he's happy.

THE OLD ESKIMO

The old Eskimo was crying his heart out; great were the poor man's troubles. A search was on to replace the mayor of this Eskimo village of five hundred people, who had just died.

"May this be your only trouble, friend!" I said. "Is there a shortage of people in the world? Choose whomever you want as your village mayor! It couldn't be that hard to run an Eskimo municipality. After all, here at God's North Pole there are no streets to be cleaned and no water works, so no mayor can be criticized for turning off the water! You have no automobile or traffic problems, no thieves to bother the police, and no factories to pollute the air! This is God's Pole! Six months of darkness, six of daylight. No electricity, no buses! So what would you do with a town government? What's a municipality good for?"

"Basically it isn't good for anything! But we still want it."

"Very well, what are you troubling yourself for, Dad? Choose somebody from the village and get it over with."

"Impossible!"

"Why impossible? Is there a law against it?"

"It's just impossible. Our mayor has to be a white man. We don't want an Eskimo mayor!"

"Good Lord! Among all these Eskimos, couldn't you find one good one to elect to serve as mayor? Are all these people bad? Isn't there a good one who knows his business?"

"There is! There has to be! Look, let me explain it to you!" said the old Eskimo, and he did:

Our village is in the north, very far north, at the mouth of a small cove. We live in an endless whiteness between two lofty rocks;

The Old Eskimo

earth is rock, sky is rock. It seems to us as if we'll be crushed between the sky and earth. For centuries, our fathers have been born, grown, gone hunting, rubbed noses, and, passing away to the darkness, disappeared from this village. No one knows how they lived. Their lives are in neither our folk songs nor our tales. In my childhood, I never heard from the old ones of that time any story at all concerning our ancestors. One would think they passed away in happiness. In fact, our forefathers died in nothingness and poverty. No one knows how or why they lived!

Until recently, there was a completely boring social order. We lived the long winter without being angry, swearing, or getting upset with anyone. There was no flavor or taste to life. It was as if we were not like a village at all, but a crowd gathered in the street! We had no social love, no social hate. If someone died in the next igloo, we felt neither pleased nor sorry. But we're not that way anymore! We can't get enough flavor out of life! The old mayor taught us all this. He gave our lives color and taught us anger and hate.

On a sweet summer day, when everyone basked in the beautiful sunshine in front of his own igloo, trying to forget the winter darkness, a crazy racket broke out in the distance, a noise too weird for words. A white man on a snowmobile was coming toward our village. He was of the race of government men from the cities in the south, a white man. He got off the vehicle. I greeted him. He called the village elders to him.

"Who is the mayor of this village?" he asked.

"The what?"

"Mayor of the municipality."

"What's a mayor for?" we asked.

"Municipality means government. The mayor keeps your streets clean. He provides you with water. He controls the traffic in your streets. He performs marriages. The municipality is government; it collects taxes!"

"We have no need for a municipality," we said. "We have no streets to be cleaned. There's water in front of every igloo, thank God! Then, we have our own girls. We marry our own."

The man became angry at this.

The Old Eskimo

"All right!" he said, "I'll appoint myself mayor! I'll help take you to a more advanced state of civilization. I'll open a school for your village. I'll establish a church for you here. I'll illuminate your long dark winter. From now on, there is a suspension of disease, and henceforth, those who are sick will not remain hungry."

That winter, as mayor, he governed us very well. First, however, he ordered a big igloo built for himself. Those who objected, he encouraged to work by beating them with a razor strop. After his igloo was finished, he gathered all the village notables and shared his thoughts with us.

"I have been among you a few days as your guest," he said. "I've noticed that your way of life is very backward. You don't know what's going on in the world. You are all grossly ignorant! Just look at this village! You have neither a municipality nor taxes. You live the way prehistoric, primitive societies did. I will save you from this condition. As my first act, I have elected myself mayor. Are there any opposed? None, are there? Fine! Now I want two assistants."

The mayor asked who the strongest man in the village was, and we gave him the names of two young men. He chose them as his helpers. Thus the white man founded the first government.

Three or four days later, the mayor set up a trading post. He sold us everything we needed. But we had no money to pay! So the man created his own money. He used playing cards for money. He distributed the new money to us as a loan and we paid it off with the skins of wolves and seals we had killed. Due to his coercion, our village experienced an organized life for the first time. He published appropriate laws for us. He forbade having bowel movements just any old place. It was dirty and would make us sick. When they asked, "What about those who have the urge in the wilds?" he sold bowel movement indulgences for money. The fellow even tied a crap in the wilds to money!

With him in charge, laziness in the village decreased. We had to work in order to pay taxes. He put everyone in the race, and our people were happy with the new situation. They worked and worked! In a short time, laziness disappeared. True, the young people were a little angry at this, but the mayor's strong helpers straight-

The Old Eskimo

ened them out. It took very little roughing-up for them to quickly behave themselves.

That long winter passed nicely and pleasantly. First we gave prayers of gratitude to our mayor. Then we loaded the responsibility of evil on him. When the weather was bad, we asked him to correct it. When old people became sick, we expected him to make them well. Naturally, when he couldn't do these things, we became angry and cursed the man. When we swore, we enjoyed the flavor of swearing. When I swore at this white man, my love for the Eskimo beside me grew. I was aware that he had high cheekbones and slanted eyes like mine. The white man began to seem ugly to me. In addition, we became aware that he cheated us with the products he sold in his store.

Suddenly, we realized this man was giving us a hard time. He didn't do a thing, just poured out orders from where he sat. The man had everything he wanted, he lacked for nothing; one hand in honey, the other in butter. He married three pretty village girls, too. "That's the custom!" he said. "The mayor has to have many wives." In a short time, the mayor possessed hundreds of wolf and seal pelts. He collected these, took them south to sell and in their place brought us necessary—or unnecessary—things. On his last return he brought a flock of cheap jewelry. He distributed these to the girls and women and thus put us in debt for skins. Then he brought medicines. He sold pills to the sick. Some of them got well, some died. Even worse, if we sneezed, he either fined us or sold us medicine. Everyone was up to his neck in debt. He didn't let us catch our breath!

At last we reached a decision. We were going to oust the white man but we didn't quite know how to do it. "Let's kill him!" we said, knowing that would never do. The man had really scared us. He was God's beloved servant! Whoever killed him would meet with a great catastrophe! "Throw him to the wolves! Let's throw him out of the village!" A few of us talked like this and got beat up. He had addicted some of us to "dream cigarettes." Those who smoked them "went on a trip." These addicts did whatever he said and never opposed him. A curse beyond words...

The Old Eskimo

Finally, one summer day, we awoke to find the man had flown the coop. He had collected all his furs and left. We took a deep breath. At last we were saved! We were happy and declared a holiday. The village elders gathered and decided that henceforth the mayor would be an Eskimo. We chose from among us the most intelligent and knowledgeable man to be mayor. That winter, things went well. Taxes and forced labor ceased. Life became boring. No one was vindictive. A looseness developed in everyone. No one went hunting. We became accustomed to laziness. We were about to die of hunger in the near future. No one would cheat us again. Gossip in the village ceased. The meaning of life quickly disappeared. The young again were bored. With no taxes to pay, there was no pleasure in working. When one or two of the younger ones took their wives and children to another cove to establish a new village, we saw that this couldn't go on. We had to have someone to cheat and prod us! It seemed to us that the most difficult thing was to live without lies.

Previously, when we were bored, we went to the mayor and listened to his lies. What beautiful, what sweet promises he used to give us! "I will bring you heat and light so you may spend the winter in comfort. I will save you all from the evil winter!" he used to say. "The day will come when sickness will end. Your troubles will be over and you will live in happiness without hunting, without working!" He promised health to the sick. He promised young bachelors two wives each. We all listened to these things in rapture. We knew they were lies but, still, listening to them was beautiful.

Truly, the long winter nights don't pass without lies. "Only such dreams can diminish the great darkness without and within a man," we said. We brought this trouble on ourselves, down on our own heads. Stupidly we threw away the easy life! It bored and distressed us to live straight. Now we can't live without falsehood! We had the lying and cheating sickness. But for us, it wasn't a lie, it was a dream! It was hope! We needed a trickster with a sweet tongue to diminish our darkness!

We went to the city and brought back a man fresh out of prison to be our mayor. Unfortunately, the stupid fellow died a few days age. He left us without a mayor again. The worst thing is that no one wants to come to God's North Pole country. That's luck for you.

The Old Eskimo

So once more we're searching for a trickster with a smooth tongue and a great capacity for deception to govern us.

SUICIDE IN NEW YORK

My Swiss friend, Henri, talked about going to New York, complaisant as the elephants who sense they are going to die and make their way to secret graves. "I'm bored with life," he said, a bottle of beer in his hand. "It's lost all attraction! That good-for-nothing wife won't give me a divorce. 'I'm fed up!' I tell her. 'I'm not,' she replies, indifferently. 'Come on, it won't work on just your desires,' I say, but she won't listen! The wife says, 'I get divorced only once every three years and we've been married only two. I haven't had enough of this marriage yet.' Damn her! Immoral, disagreeable shrew! So she isn't bored! 'I'm fed up with living in the same house and sleeping in the same bed with you. What's more, I'm not going to play cabin boy any longer. Friendship's over! Let's break up the partnership! I go my way, you go yours. You're on your own. Go with anyone you like. Just leave me alone! Leave me alone so I can find a bride I enjoy, one who's useful and more to my taste. Come on; I'm running around idle with nothing to do. Is your hanging on to me like a leach really proper? Stop hounding me!'

"I've been broke for three months. Not a dime in my pocket! The wife pays the rent and food. I don't have even a penny to spend! I tell her, 'Let me go, see how much money you'll save'; but she says, 'No, impossible! I don't mind. Don't work, stay at home!' What a stinking mess. Man, the things that happen to me..."

Without stopping or listening, Henri told his story; he was troubled. Henri was disgusted with his life. I had never expected my old neighbor to come to this state of affairs. He was an active, cheerful man. I ordered Henri another beer. "My trouble isn't only my wife. Unemployment is killing me! All day, I stay home and get fed like a breeding bull. The wife comes, goes, and crams food into me. She checks on me and if I don't eat properly, she cuts off my pocket money. Or she says, 'All right, off to bed!' You can't live around here without money! Then, she's after me to make love night and day! She can't get enough, she's insatiable, the tart!

"It can't go on like this," Henri continued. "Only death can cleanse this filth!"

I told him, "Come on, give up this wish! You're a young man. You have a beautiful young wife. Furthermore, she loves you. She doesn't care about your unemployment nor your bad manners. Is there any sense in saddening the poor woman with your talk about suicide?"

Henri's expression was very serious. He had the look of a person who had made a firm decision. "Tomorrow, without fail, I'll carry out my suicide plan," he said.

"Just tell me," I asked Henri, "how are you going to do it?"

"This weekend I'll go to New York."

"Good God! Is it sweeter to die in New York? If you're going to die, die here; what sense is there in taking this business to New York? It would put us to a lot of expense. We would have to send wreaths to New York. Come on, give up this wish! However, if you really intend to commit suicide, do it here in Montreal! The bottom line is death, isn't it? What's the matter with Montreal? Grave plots are very expensive in New York; you'll cause a lot of trouble. Then, if you decide on suicide and accidentally don't die, the city will realize you're not going to be in a position to pay the grave and burial costs, so they'll take you to court for fraud. You'd go to jail for nothing, my dear friend. It's nothing, but this business will harm us, too. You think that for the sake of your beautiful wife, it's necessary to go all the way to New York? Come on, get off it! If you're going to die, die here! Whatever God-awful thing, do it here! Pick a day in the middle of the week. Then we won't lose our Saturday and Sunday but can take a weekday off."

"No!" said Henri. "That won't do. Listen to me! I'm a coward. There's no possibility that I can kill myself. I can neither blow my brains out with a pistol nor open a bloody hole like a red rose in my chest. I can't take sleeping pills and kill myself. God damn it, it's impossible for me to go to bed with the wife and sleep, either.

Suicide in New York

I can't climb a high hill and jump—I'm afraid of heights! The best way is to go to New York," he maintained.

Then Henri asked me, "Have you ever been to New York?"

I looked at him in surprise. "No."

"America's most beautiful city, New York!" he said. "Living in New York takes a special skill. It's not something everyone can do. Just as it's necessary to be a fish to live in the sea, have wings in order to fly in the air, to live in New York you must be a New Yorker. New Yorkers are not like us, they were created as another breed. For example, their lungs are not purified with oxygen; carbon dioxide is needed. And the silence of the countryside makes a New Yorker sick. He can't stand it! Great size and crowds are necessary for New Yorkers.

"Not everyone can be a New Yorker! Not everyone is naturally endowed with the ability to live in that city. It's difficult for provincials. That's why provincial Americans, who have decided on suicide, spend a weekend in New York. This is the cleanest, the easiest kind of death. And the most fun. Oh, mother! You die joyfully! Exhausted with joy, you give up the ghost. Those who live in New York don't smile. You only see provincials die laughing with joy. It's very reliable; all those who go there to commit suicide, die! Naturally, you can't buy death, so money's no advantage; you have to wait your turn. Sometimes it comes early, sometimes late. If you're lucky, you'll fart your last immediately. There was an unlucky provincial who lived on in misery for twenty years. Last weekend—long life to you!—his turn came. But, for that waiting period he was never bored. He enjoyed his twenty-year wait. That's why I've decided I'm going to New York.

"Let me tell you how I'm going to do this business. Listen! This is going to be the nicest of all the deaths you've ever seen. It will start like this: On a beautiful Saturday, I start out in an old Cadillac. The roads shine, it's four wide lanes each way, like heaven. Trees emerald green, birds singing in the trees ... The highway to New York is filled with cars, bumper to bumper, all speeding like lightning. I have youth in my blood. Oh, mother! Step on the gas! The car's out of control, I'm out of control! The car flies through the air, I stay behind! I adhere to the pavement as if I were embracing a

Suicide in New York

young girl. Life is beautiful! OK, friend, I'm done for! According to the figures, mobs of people surrender their souls to God every Saturday on the highways. If you're young, a bachelor, you drink, and your car's old, God doesn't hesitate long before taking your soul. So here's a guaranteed suicide for you! Well, let's say there was a hitch, I didn't get my soul snatched and I arrived in New York . . .

"Being a bachelor in New York is truly another pleasure! The city's an amusement park from one end to the other. The hotels, the streets are filled to the brim with people. Whatever door in New York you open, people pour out just like boxes from Fibber McGee's closet. You even have to be careful when you open the closet door in your own house! That's no joke! You can even meet with an attack from people getting off the train.

"It's hard to find a hotel. Every place is filled with provincials bent on suicide. One way to achieve this is to walk the streets. It will come about from some memorable incident involving a mugger or an automobile accident.

"New Yorkers are very lovable people. On the streets, in the parks, they're always intimate, friendly, and locked in close embrace. Their blood is fiery. Love and brotherhood spring forth from New Yorkers' eyes and faces. You can ask directions from any man or girl in the streets or, just to make conversation, inquire as to the name of a food. You say, 'Fine, you're just the person to do a job for me!' and from then on this sincere friend will follow you until you die. New Yorkers are truly obliging people. They have great respect for tourists. They don't want tourists bent on suicide to leave before they succeed. After all, the city's income is based on this!

"But suppose this scheme didn't work out, either. New York's surprises never end. Everything is arranged to confuse a person. In spite of the city's size, nothing ever breaks down. Everything works like a clock. One is never bored even for a minute. Strikes occur on time. The electricity is cut off right to the exact second. The trains and subways are late without exception. For this reason, there is no possibility of going to any program at the wrong time. As soon as I arrive in the city, I'll take a room on the top floor of a big hotel. During summer in the city, the electricity is off most of the time. The elevators don't operate. Just think about me climbing forty or

Suicide in New York

fifty stories. Undoubtedly, I'll arrive at the next world from heart failure. The water will be cut off. The toilets won't flush. The windows won't open or close. In the city there's every contrary thing in the world needed to drive a man crazy!

"However, let's say that things go wrong, that I don't die, go crazy, or get killed in an accident. The next evening I go out to see this interesting city. The city lights and colors blind a man. The neon lights tell a thousand and one stories. Riches and plenty flash on every side. Wait, it's July, isn't it? Don't be surprised. Every July the garbage men are on strike. Five tons of manure and garbage accumulate per day in the street. It's impassable because of flies, stink, and filth. Look around! Rats raid the streets and boulevards. From these smells, if nothing else, you'll die as if from poison gas. Don't worry about the New Yorkers' lives. Remember, I told you, they are different creatures.

"You want entertainment, some excitement? You came to the right place, friend! Women, girls, carousing—all are here. Heroin, cocaine, alcohol, gambling at your beck and call! They stop a man on the corner and ask after his health. 'How are you?' they ask, then they offer you two-dollar cigarettes. Even if they insist, say no and don't smoke one! Before you could light up the police would sprout up right in front of you. Better to fall into the hands of Azrael, the Angel of Death, than the New York police. Is there a better place for suicide than this?"

MILL STREET STRIKE

Mill Street in Montreal extends east and west toward the docks. Flanked by warehouses storing exotic goods, it smells like a spice bazaar rather than an ordinary street. At one end stands the public entrance to the harbor, at the other, a flour mill; to the south flows the St. Lawrence River, frozen into a block of ice in winter, a secret stream in summer, invisible under ships and birds.

Farmers from surrounding villages bring their daughters in white stockings and clean aprons to Montreal in the summertime to show them this great river.

Between eight in the morning and six at night giant trucks fill Mill Street. These vehicles, as long as eight automobiles, hum along light as a feather. Small, sparkling-clean private cars, calling with their horns, tease and make fun of the big trucks. An automobile winding up on this road is like a gentleman wearing a bow tie in a slum neighborhood, a misfit, out of place.

Every morning, cars coming from the South Shore turn left as soon as they cross the iron bridge and block Mill Street from one end to the other. Filled with dirt and spicy smells, Mill Street is alive with derisive, rude drivers.

Evenings, in a layer of superfine pink dust, the street becomes isolated, silent and calm. Other than a night watchman or two and a head looking from a window, nothing is visible on Mill Street . . .

One Monday, the street came suddenly alive. It was teeming with people and workers with placards. Laborers flowed into Mill Street from every direction, like water accumulating from snowmelt in the mountains. Quietly, slowly, all the workers in the city gathered there.

Mill Street Strike

On a previous morning, when seven elevator operators from the harbor awakened, to save themselves from boredom and have a little fun, they found it fitting to request a fifteen percent increase in their pay. After having breakfast, they increased their demands to twenty percent.

Management found the twenty percent high and sent their request back. Monday morning at eight, the seven elevator operators, after a nice breakfast, took positions at the public entrance to the harbor at the foot of Mill Street, carrying placards, to go on strike.

In the sweet freshness of morning, the seven elevator operators were thinking only of the high cost of living, increasing expenses, and their decreasing incomes. Milk, sugar, cheese, and beer had become very expensive. Rent had gone up and airplane tickets had gone sky-high. The price of cigarettes and clothing was out of sight. In one year the cost of living had gone up eleven percent. The twenty percent raise would provide them nine percent extra. Under present-day conditions, this was a natural request.

In order to provide protection for the seven workers, two police officers, after breakfasting together with the operators that Monday morning, took up their duties.

The first day passed without incident. The second day, because they needed the elevator operators to carry their cleaning equipment, the harbor toilet cleaners joined the strike.

Tuesday, those sixteen harbor toilet cleaners, carrying placards, took up their positions, distant from the seven operators. The elevator operators disliked the toilet cleaners. They maintained their distance because of the cleaners' filthy smell.

Life otherwise in Mill Street proceeded normally. Great trucks flew from left to right like carefree swallows.

On Wednesday, the workers who continued to work at the harbor became greatly annoyed. Toilets were dirty. By evening the whole place stank of urine and feces. Angry female employees decided to go on strike Thursday if the toilet issue were not resolved.

So on Thursday, eighty-two secretaries, telephone operators, and other female employees, placards in hand, took their posts beside the other workers, in protest of the injustice done them. Of the eighty-two female employees, thirty-two wore miniskirts. Forty were middle-aged and homely. Ten were elderly. Only two of the eighty-two female employees were virgins. Eighty-one owned automobiles. One was African Canadian.

Thursday morning, the Montreal Police Department assigned thirty police officers to provide protection for the more than one hundred strikers. The Red Cross provided two pickup trucks to distribute hot tea and coffee.

Thirty-two managers and sixty-seven assistant managers, whose telephones were not being answered and who remained without morning coffee, both in order to reinforce the rights and desires of the workers and also to find a solution to rising inflation, suddenly decided to strike.

At this time, in the harbor, three freighters, sailing under the British flag, were waiting their turns to load grain for India. A telegram from India stated that the food situation was bad and requested that the wheat be loaded as soon as possible; that otherwise some hundreds of thousands would die of hunger.

After the managers and assistant managers decided to strike, 1,659 dock workers, perhaps in hope they could get something out of it, found it fitting to join the other strikers. Friday at nine, they joined the picket line.

Friday, at twelve o'clock noon, work over the entire harbor came to a halt. That afternoon, the strike committee denied permission to a Hungarian passenger ship for passengers to go ashore.

Life on Mill Street completely stopped. Big trucks lay stretched out in the streets like dead buffalo. Other than white doves, nothing moved. Thus seven days passed, one week.

The people of Montreal considered the strike a useful tool.

Workers on the railroad that carried wheat to the harbor, on the second Monday, fearing that they would be out of work and looking for a way to solve the high cost of living, found it fitting to decide to strike. Tuesday, twenty thousand rail workers joined in. The Montreal rail network ceased operation. Locomotives pulled into the sheds. Nothing came or went.

Wednesday, members of the Highway Transportation Union, who thought to take advantage of this situation and who had for a long time hoped to achieve the working hours they wanted, decided to strike. The thirty-thousand-member union went on vacation.

Thursday, all the city's fruit and vegetables were exhausted. A food shortage appeared. The Construction and Builders Union, two hundred twenty thousand members, who were unhappy with this situation, walked off the job.

Friday, the Montreal Olympic Building Committee, by means of letters to iron, steel, cement, lumber, and tile factories, asked cancellation of some purchase orders due to the strike.

Another seven days had passed, the second week.

All Canada regarded the strike as a useful action.

During the third week, the iron, cement, lumber, and tile factories went on strike. When the unemployed factory workers' buying power decreased, sales of other factories also fell. The strike slowly spread to other factories. All Canada turned into a vacant, silent city park with flower beds . . .

Now the harbor was filled with ships. Two freighters, which had come to load wheat for Red China, took their places among the seagulls, coquettishly as brides. The Montreal firemen and police, finding it fitting to join their brother workers, also decided to strike.

For a time, the religious services in Montreal churches continued as usual. Thieves, pickpockets, and bank robbers grew quite weary; taking advantage of the lack of police and working overtime, they had robbed many banks and citizens.

Finally, newspaper workers went on strike. They neglected to inform the penniless Montreal workers that two hundred fifty thousand poor and hungry died in India. Montreal had ceased to be concerned about the outside world.

Three weeks after the beginning of the strike, the situation was as follows:

The whole city, of one heart, insisted on the strike to protect the rights of the seven workers, in spite of hell or high water. The entire city was without bread or milk, sugar, and beer. Everyplace swam in filth. Yet no one felt any remorse.

On Monday of the fourth week, paralyzed, Montreal City published a decree with the aim of restoring order and providing that the strikers go back to work.

Mill Street Strike

Tuesday, the heroic workers decided to continue the strike with its aim of securing and protecting their God-given rights.

Wednesday, the government announced in tough language that those who didn't conform to the published decree would be punished severely.

Thursday, with the intention of learning whether or not the government decree was constitutional, the workers applied to the Supreme Court.

Friday and Saturday, nothing happened.

Sunday, the government and workers took advantage of the beautiful weather and prepared picnic lunches. In the open air, soccer and volleyball were played, stories were told.

One spring evening, a strange smell enveloped Mill Street, the odor of burning leaves. As a wisp of smoke rose toward the sky, small children from the poor neighborhood ran to see.

Leaves were burning. Little red flames crackled among the leaves and progressed toward a nearby house. A boy urinated on the flames to put them out, then all the boys joined him. But the flames caught on the house's wooden siding. The house went up like a torch.

First, the firemen quit their strike and ran to help. The police joined them. After that, the railroad workers, dock workers, then the managers and their assistants, female employees, toilet cleaners, and finally the seven elevator operators broke their strike and ran to help.

Monday, the city was cleaned. The ships were loaded with wheat and the two hundred fifty thousand who had died of hunger in India came back to life. . . .

AGALUK

All was green in the rays of the low-lying sun, green as fresh grass. At sunset, the ice turned beet red, then became the light blue of sea and sky. Mountains of ice . . .

White polar bears, northern owls, seals, and Eskimos lived on the plain in the vicinity of a hill that lay like a woman with a swollen belly.

Mornings, Agaluk awakened with the cascades of white that surrounded him. Water, the daylight hummed. Polar hares, caribou awakened when the wild wind blew. Dry wood popped, cracked, separated, contracted, and darkness disappeared.

Agaluk arose from where he lay like a pole. He got to his feet. From the distance, from the sunless dawn, the river of light flowed, became liquid, spread; the earth dissolved into the sky. The light wet the earth in patches and lit the sky. Everything shone. It was morning.

Agaluk went out of his igloo into the void. As far as he could see was whiteness, snow. Freedom was great and widespread. The freedom he loved! He loved this endless white struggle; he rubbed his hands together. It was marvelous to live as an Eskimo.

Polar bears, winter's hungry wolves, wind deer, sly fish merged with Eskimos, became snow, and fell as one. They became water, then froze together. "A smooth way of life is a sweet life," Agaluk said. Life here had remained like that of a falcon. When hungry, the Eskimo ate the bear, rabbit, fish, or dog. If the bear was hungry, he ate old Eskimos, rabbits, and caribou. When thirsty they all drank water, they breathed pure air. Death claimed the Eskimo whose work was finished. Later, the one who died returned. In the

Agaluk

Eskimo's language there were no descriptive additions from his imagination; no one colored what he saw and knew.

Agaluk loved where he lived. He also felt inside him a great love for Eskimos. He knew well all that he loved. Light would shine on his village.

That morning, he was going to guide tourists who were coming to see village life. The places to be toured included twenty-three igloos clustered on the south bank of a small fjord occupied by nearly a hundred Eskimo men, women, and children, two small hills, and the shore of a sea filled with seals. Well, that's the whole thing, an hour tour and it's all over.

Agaluk was angry at the tourists. Why do these imbecilic Southerners come here in the first place? Don't they have any other place to go see? These parts aren't suitable for Southerners. They are desolate! There's nobody here, not a soul! Poor! Empty! The emptiness is filled with wind, light, or darkness. This place is ours! The Southerner should stay south. He shouldn't come here and corrupt the Eskimo. When the docile Eskimo sees Southerners, he changes. He corrodes like copper. And the Southerner brings his evil spirits with him, too.

Men tourists, with their dog harness on their necks, are after photographs. They watch how Eskimos hunt seal in the fjords. The freckle-faced, matchstick-legged women with skinny butts tour igloos on the hill.

After the tour, Agaluk took all the tourists to the canteen. He told them stories of seals and polar bears. The men preferred stories filled with adventure; the women, stories filled with love. But at the canteen, Agaluk said, "I sell tea, not stories!" He served hot tea to the tourists.

This is what Agaluk related:

"On the day I saw and touched earth for the first time on the shore of the quiet sea in the south, I was much afraid. I couldn't understand what it was, this earth. At first, I thought it as hot as fire or pepper. There in the south, they laughed at me." At this moment, the listening guests also laughed. Agaluk continued:

"When I saw the leaves sprout and the buds blossom into colored flowers, I was filled with excitement. In joy, I tried to eat the

Agaluk

earth. I thought it would be sweet as sugar. I asked the colors' names one by one. I looked in amazement at trees reaching for clouds. They had a hard time stopping me from eating dirt."

Agaluk stopped talking and served tea again. He said it would snow the next day.

"Tell," said the guests, "tell us more!"

"I had never seen that much color. In the Eskimo tongue there are ten words for 'white.' The name for white changes in every kind of light. I asked for the different names such as young-girl earth, woman earth, pregnant earth, night earth, and day earth, but they said they were all the same. When I saw the earth was all bare, I felt like crying. 'Does earth have a spirit?' I asked. The Southerners said it didn't. 'Is earth alive?' I asked. They said it was. 'Does earth die?' I asked. They said it doesn't. 'In that case, earth is God,' I said. Our gods are alive, without spirits, and immortal."

The guests laughed.

Agaluk, his eyes narrowed, measured the depth of the guests one by one, like a diver. "These sinners made God miserable," he said to himself.

"Do you know what ice is?" he asked the visitors. "You mix water with a stiff wind to make ice. Wind does not like fire, therefore, when it sees fire it flees and leaves the water behind. Let me serve you each another tea," he said.

He served them each another tea. "Drink, it's good." This time the tea tasted different. The visitors said, "Tell a story!" Agaluk's wolf-eyes glittered.

"Earth must be God! But who came and spread God like that on the ground? He was trod underfoot. You trampled him. You humiliated him.

"He gave you color over and over again without anger, without getting tired of it. He brought you light and trees. From his fingernails, from his leaves, beauty poured forth and you closed your eyes."

The guests were in good spirits. "Tell!" they cried, "Tell us more!"

"This was not the God of Light. The God of Light was truer, stronger. He couldn't stay in one place like a child. Now he was here, now there. He was a bird who flew. Earth wasn't like that. He was

Agaluk

a wizard. He burned incense. No one saw him, but he saw everyone. This wasn't the God of Light.

"Earth wasn't the God of Darkness either. Darkness was a caribou. He came slowly. Ponderously, he descended from the hills. Then suddenly he fled when he saw light. He was as weightless as fog. He was cold, the God of Darkness. He was colorless. He bathed with light and was cleansed. Earth was not the God of Darkness.

"This God of Earth loved the Southerners more than he loved us. He gave them everything, but the Southerners oppressed him.

"This Earth was a confused God. He lay side by side with water. I've seen all your land and water. I saw them lying together.

"This earth must be the God of Man. And like him, he never knew what he did. He loved the ones who tortured him."

Again Agaluk fell silent.

The visitors laughed. Time was passing beautifully for them at the Pole. Agaluk sold another round of tea and collected the money. The tea was bitter.

"Long, long ago, there lived a creature here who was half-girl and half-fish. She was a very generous being who helped everyone. One day people found this half-human, half-fish dead. For two days they mourned, then they forgot."

The visitors asked, "Why did this creature die?" Agaluk laughed. "Because God was stupid," he said. "He made a being that could live neither on land nor on sea. Then we village people prayed to God never to make such a foolish creature again."

The visitors were silent.

"That's how your God of Earth is. Stupid! What he gives birth to in the spring, he kills in the winter. Then, you too kill your God of Earth. You also will die one day."

They drank another bitter tea.

The next day the Southerner tourists awoke in an entirely different world.

Agaluk's God laughed that morning.

MONTREAL ... MONTREAL ...

A bad love song divides the city in two. Two sides, two different worlds. On one side, the rich, spoiled English; on the other side, eighteenth-century French Quebecois, Canucks, whose speech is unintelligible. As for the rest, there's St. Lawrence Street, which no one gives a damn about, with its whorehouses, dives, and polite drunks, who don't always refrain from yelling.

This street starts in the south, at the harbor, which smells of moss and seaweed in summer. In winter it's a noisy whistle, high-pitched and long. At the end of summer, the whores and drunks disperse as if the show is over and the stage lights have gone out. The street is deserted. It stretches thirty miles to the north. Freight trains from many nations, many civilizations, pass by.

Southern Chinese dives ... In narrow alleys that fork right and left, naked Chinese girls fill the bright show windows of run-down buildings. One night, you must come and see the girls with their narrow waists, slanting eyes, melon breasts, and tanned bodies. Race horses in heat! Potent, radiant, and ready!

May comes all at once and becomes June. Acacias come down from Kavaklidere and bloom. The smell of Ankara is in my nostrils. I have an intense longing for the green that descends from Çankaya to Kizilay and the trees that change to red in the fall. On the St. Lawrence there is a razor wind, but my heart's in mild Ankara.

Almond-eyed Chinese swarm about, taking short steps, looking absent-minded. On the inner streets, there are three or four grocery stores that sell Far-Eastern foods, many restaurants, too. Exotic Chinese music fills the Chinese quarter hidden under the shadows of skyscrapers. Isolation, poverty, indifference, dust, and dirt in summer; in winter, gray snow.

Montreal . . . Montreal . . .

All of the Far-Eastern artists gather in a small gallery adjacent to the San Lu Restaurant, at the end of the street. As soon as one enters the door, one sees on the wall fishermen's boats, the sleepy China Sea—blue-green, deep, across from the setting sun, reflecting inner silence. A heavy odor of grass draws me to the China Sea. Suddenly, I am in three places: near the acacias cascading down the Turkish Ministry of Agriculture Building, on the quiet China sea which has become a lake, and outside in Montreal's razor-sharp wind . . .

The owner of the gallery is the president of the Canada Chinese Culture Association. "Are there many Turks in Montreal?" he asked me. "How are Turkish painters? Do you have good artists?"

"We have!" I answered. "They are progressive; they reflect Turkey's realities. I've brought a few pictures with me to be framed."

"Let me see them."

I showed him the paintings.

"Very nice!" he said. "What is this one?"

"*Wedding on the Sea.*"

Keskinok's work remains unfamiliar here.

The Chinese looked at me, waiting for further explanation. Then he said, "A nice painting." He examined another work, a watercolor, the subject *Migration in the Snow*. He read the name, Erol, correctly. "A powerful artist!" he remarked. I nodded my head. He didn't have the frames I wanted.

I looked at a work that portrayed, between two blooming almond branches, a snowy mountain with dark green valleys beyond.

"*Far-off Spring,*" said the Chinese. "I'll sell it cheap if you want it." There was an artist's language in the shop that I couldn't understand or speak. Its color, expression, and message were unfamiliar to me.

When I left the gallery, the Chinese said, "Come again, Turk!" It felt like a rainy, gray day, but outside it was dry as a bone. While changing from fall to winter, planet earth just goes from bad to worse.

I stopped in front of the Hungarian Art Gallery with its broad windows. Displayed was a bust of Kennedy. The gallery owner was Pol Lanz, a Hungarian sculptor with wild, bristling hair. He said, "Whose paintings do you have?"

"Turkish artists."

"If you're partial to watercolors, I have a few works of Hungarian artists. If you like them, I'll sell them cheap. Twenty dollars each. You 'Töröks' occupied us for a hundred fifty years."

Pol said Török for Turk as they do in Hungary. "We learned business tricks from you," he said. "You know any rich people? I'm looking for art lovers who want a bust done. You look like someone with lots of acquaintances. Find me a couple of customers."

He looked at the pictures I had with me. "Who's this Abak?" he asked.

"Not Abak, *Abaç*," I said, "a Török like me!"

"Hmmm! Good artist!" he said. "Who's this Nüzhet? He Török too?"

"Yes."

"This good too. OK, what kind of frames you want for these? Leave them in my show window a few days. These good artists. Is there good artists in Turkey?"

"There are!"

"Our Hungarian artists are good too, but . . . I just can't sell them. You going to open a show with these?"

"Perhaps," I said and left the paintings at the gallery.

On the left, in front of the theater school, a drunken street girl let out a whopping yell. She must have been angry about something. Lebanese Haddad's grocery store was a little farther on. He has the best *kaşar* cheese, hot *sucuk* sausage and smuggled *Zahle* raki. He also carries rose water and mountain thyme.

Then, on the right, the Acropolis Restaurant. On Sundays they roast *döner*, pressed lamb on a vertical spit. The street is filled with short, swarthy, fearful, chilled immigrants. All come from sunny, warm countries. The sunshine of bright, blue-skied Athens, whitewashed Lisbon, Rome, Beirut, and Alexandria shines on their faces.

But what about the acacias from Kavakli?

I returned the way I came. Two Chinese had their entire attention focused on the Hungarian Art Gallery show window. In the window were two autumn scenes from Bahçelievler. A huge sea goddess. Blue-white waters of the Mediterranean moving gently with all their subtle shadings. I watched the Chinese, listened as they spoke in singsong syllables. The blood leaped in my brain. Such ignorance! Damn son-of-a-Chinaman. This artist's name is Abaç, not Abak! This is Erol, Keskinok, that's Nüzhet, that's Büyükişliyen, this is Gökçebağ . . .

On St. Lawrence Street one can yell and swear all he wants and that's what I did. The gray of fall tasted like quinine in my mouth. I had to spit it out.

The two Chinese looked at the man spouting nonsense. They smiled, then walked away. I yelled after them, "Take a good look, dummies! At least there's some sunshine and color there. Bastards! You can keep your naked Chinese girls—and your neighborhood, too. . . ."

DESERT

I told my neighbor, "We Indians first discovered sweetness. Yours is false, ours is genuine and good. We enjoyed sun, woman, lake, and rain. In mountain darkness, by the light of a wood fire, we found sweetness." I told her, "A naked woman's plump-filly calves, fish-wet breasts, and rabbit-scared eyes are honey. We love woman with our hands, growling and gnawing flesh from her bones with our teeth. When loved, she is honey, sweetness."

I told my neighbor, "Night for you is a starless city night, a meager night! You're left horseless in a dark valley. You're an ant. You don't know where you came from or where you're going."

My neighbor got good and mad. "Dirty, stupid redskin!" she said. I laughed. She got even madder. When angry she became alive and I knew her better. A wounded beaver, she had no place to go.

"The things you love are sour!" I said. "The sour smell of rotten fish. Your love is a turtle. You can't get out of its shell."

"You're talking nonsense!" she replied. "Love can't be a turtle, a man's heart can't be night. You're ignorant."

"That's the way it is."

"You're dirty!" she said.

I had first seen her naked in the lake. In the water she was neither waterfowl nor fish. I couldn't take my eyes from the water in the moonlight. She had a long mane. Blond. There among the colorful birds and deer of the pine forest, I couldn't believe at that moment that my neighbor was a woman.

I was a summer wind—I blew gently. I rippled the water. She wasn't startled. She gleamed in the light. In the middle of the shining lake, two naked cicadas. We called out. We spoke. The days

Desert

after that fled the distance of three plains. They just flew away. They approached a little, then fled.

It rained, wetting the mountain flowers in the pine forest, then ceased.

One day when I was sick, she brought food. I didn't remain silent. "The inside of your head is a trash can!" I said. "It's filled with mixed-up, useless things."

"I won't bring you food again," she said. I laughed like a fox. "Your beauty is rotten!" I replied.

We Indians were the first to look at the delight of the skies. We made the sweetness into daylight and filtered it in our eyes.

Two yellow daisies, one deer, a tiny wind; when they're all together, the plain became sweetness. I looked into her face. "The inside of your eyes is tin-can rusty!" I said. Really, they were duck-blue.

"Why do you annoy me?" she asked. I didn't answer. I pointed at the trees. "The branches are budding." She was going to leave, but I stopped her. "Your breasts are copper," I said.

"What are my breasts to you?"

"Your flesh is the flesh of a crow, ten days dead, inedible," I said.

She was a big child, my neighbor.

"My Indian wife's breasts are apples and pears. Their tips are strawberries, blackberries. They thunder down from her shoulders like a waterfall. The tops are sunburned, the bottoms snow-white. They are bread. My wife's breasts are filly-live, filly-naked."

My young neighbor was beside herself with rage. "Do you have a wife?" she asked.

"No!"

"Very well, then, why do you tell me these things?"

"I wanted to, that's why."

She slammed the door and left.

My neighbor thought herself a woman. She was not woman but fire. "No!" I said. "When the heads of grain ripen in the fields, when the boughs bend with loaded blossoms at summer's end, then you're a woman. Now, you're a tree with sparse leaves. When they become dense, you're a woman. When you converge with your instincts, you're a woman."

She calls me "crazy, insane, penniless!" Let her say what she pleases.

"What's this?" I ask.

"Hair!"

"And this?"

"Myself!" she said.

"Well, that's all you are. But, if I say so, you're something else," I said. I expected her to reply, "I'm waiting, say on!" but she didn't. She didn't say it yet, but her day was coming.

"You have a big house with little land. You have a horse that doesn't gallop, doesn't whinny. Not a horse, you have a machine. I have lakes, wind, inexhaustible land. I have four seasons. Shall I tell you more?" She didn't answer.

We were walking side by side in the forest. I told my blond neighbor, "We were the first to taste salt." She threw her arms open like Jesus and stalked off. I yelled after her, "If you're without game in the forest, if the flowers are without wind, it's salt." Then I laughed. I knew that now she would call me a crazy Indian. Again I yelled after her, "If my wife sweats in hot sun, hot sand, among windless bushes, her lips are salty." Behind my back she called me crazy. Well, I am crazy! What's more, raving mad! After a little while she'll come back, my fire.

Twenty-one years old. I told her, "Everything about you is false. Your talk is false, your sleep is false, your love is false, what you know is false."

"Not so," she replied. "Like you, I love beauty."

"No!" I said and pointed to the city. "That's what you love. Go there!" She stopped and softened. I saw a female wolf-glint in her eyes. We communicated with smoke. She gave a signal. "All right," I thought, "almost ready."

She paced back and forth in the room two or three times. I was waiting. She would either run away or submit to the smoke signals of her heart.

She was rich. She had plenty. She did everything she wanted. She lived without duties, a horse pulling no load, a cow giving no milk, a chicken laying no eggs. A lake lily, she grew without worry. She lived alone in a big house on the lakeshore. She had no one.

Desert

She had legs longer than a horse, breasts livelier that a raw pear. She wasn't dried up like our girls. She flew, she lived. She added unheard-of color to everyone she looked at, or to nature. When she awakened, opened her eyes, her dreams didn't stop, they continued on.

Her naked body was as lovely as a garden cucumber. The whiteness of her flesh was the snow of a three-day journey. I don't look at her. She paws the ground with her forefoot, breathing heavily. In a moment she might attack me. She might whinny.

She pricks up her ears; draws near. "I'll give you a few raisins, something sweet," I say. "Have you seen the cool spring roses?"

"Which are they?"

"The ones by the gate."

"Those are tulips!" she says.

"So they're tulips. I call them cool roses because they love the cool. If the Blackfoot Indians in the west saw you, they would run in fear. They would say, 'We have never seen a cool rose this big!'"

She laughed. Her laugh became lights, one inside the other, echoing in her eyes. She approached another step.

"It's the day!" I said.

"Do you know what it is to be a female?" I asked.

"Yes!"

"The mate is the one who makes her female," I said. "The male, close to nature, makes her female."

She stood erect in front of me, looking at my face as if gazing through an open door.

"Undress!" I said.

THREE DRUNKS IN THE PARK

Long swollen buildings, scabby wounds on the sky, blistered; if scratched with fingernails they would leak and bleed.

Southeast, behind the cathedral dome, blazed a bloody sun, scorching the area.

A black funeral slowly passed by in the street, immersed in the flood of light. An idler or two retreated to the side of the road and watched. People passed by like a train, car by car, clattering and humming.

A copper redness spread through the city. The land was black, hard, pitch, flowerless.

A black child, his mother holding him firmly by the hand, screamed, weeping his heart out.

Three drunks walked toward the park. A hot September, steel-dry. Beginning rust reddened the edges of the leaves, decaying them. Autumn was coming.

Slippery-snake automobiles, bumper to bumper, flowed by in the red-steel light, starting, stopping, in jerks. Grass and flowers, like patches, filled spaces between stone buildings.

In the windless summer air, tourists dragged themselves from here to there like colored balloons.

In the sky, all had flown off, from live birds to steel planes. The sky was empty, void.

The front of the Queen Elizabeth Hotel teemed. Dominion Square Park, in the heart of the city, was filled with people who had eaten lunch. All benches were taken, all bellies were lightly puffed, eyes were sleepy. Employees in that part of town were taking a break.

The crowd was talking of the high cost of living. They were saying, "Clothes are expensive, food is high." Most of the men filling

Three Drunks in the Park

the benches wore dark-blue, striped suits. Following the laws of economics, all employees had bought the blue striped suits that were overstocked. "Life is expensive," everyone said, "very expensive!"

At a bench in the center of the park all hell broke loose. Noise, racket, laughing were heard. Three old men were sitting there. Their grimy clothes, week's growth of beard on all of them, uncombed hair, worn-out shoes, and tieless shirts attracted attention. If it had been washed, their gray hair would have been snow white. They talked noisily and yelled like schoolboys. Then they looked around to see if they were being watched.

In the dense shadows of enormous trees, the city roar was diminished and silenced. The birdless, beeless, flyless, butterflyless trees put fear into a man. The trees, overloaded with leaves, were empty of life; not a living thing was to be seen. The sky, like a wrinkled sheet, was artificial, lifeless . . .

One of the three old men sitting in the middle of the park said to his neighbor, "I used to be on the Mediterranean. Such a sea; words fail me! An enormous blue waterbed. It's not just water, it's the water of life. In it, you come alive, you're strengthened. It's not a bed of filth like your rivers."

The old man on the left said, "Yeh! I've seen the Mediterranean too. It's not at all like the other seas. Just like you said, Bob, not a sea but like a naked woman, bless her heart. It's a lively flirt, bubbling everywhere. When it's quiet, it embraces, kisses, and licks a person. If it gets angry, you've had it. You can't endure the yells of a whore."

The three old men fell silent. All three were drunk. The subject of women was one they had forgotten for a long time. "Just look at 'em!" said Al, who sat on the left. "Are these girls? They're mangy dogs. They have no life, no urges. You ought to see the girls on Mediterranean shores. They're all made of sugar, aren't they, Bob?"

Bob's eyes shone. "I'm most crazy about Mediterranean birds. Man, what birds, what birds! Forget the women and girls, now! The best part of the Mediterranean is the birds. The seashore is filled with birds; it's a bird paradise. White snow birds flying everywhere. They call them seagulls. Miles of shore, blue water. The sea runs on the shore, foams, then somehow turns into seagulls and flies."

Three Drunks in the Park

Drunken Al, sitting on the left, made rude remarks at passing girls.

Bob continued, "That's the Mediterranean for you; like no other sea. It's like a fan—every two minutes, the white end of the sea turns into a bird and flies. The water is so warm and salty you wouldn't believe it. Man, we rot around here! You call this the world? Look at that sun! A deathbed! Look at the land! Pitch! How about the damn birds in these trees? None, are there? If you want birds they're at the Mediterranean. What sweet voices they have! So in harmony with the rustle of the sea!"

Al said to Bob, "Tell us more about the seagulls! In World War II, I was in southern France. I had a young sweetheart. One day I took her to the seashore. I undressed my sweetheart among the birds. Now, when you talk about birds, I see that nude sweetheart in front of my eyes. When you're quiet, the image disappears. How beautiful she was, that French girl. Like you said, Bob! Just like you were telling. Her hair flew in the warm wind. When the wind blew, the birds took to flight. Her skirts flew like the birds. She had tiny white panties. Red hot, like a seagull!

"That day, war, woman, sea, love were all together. The memories are all alive now. Oh man! How sweet it was, those days. Come on, Bob, tell us about the seagulls, tell us again!"

At that moment, those three drunks in the park were living again a war brought forth from the grave. Inside the park all came to life. To the three drunks, the birds who had disappeared since morning had now come back. They were chirping all around. The empty-faced girls had sweetened in an instant. They were skipping like seagulls. Al looked at the girls. "Look!" he said, "Just look at these French beauties! They'll drive you wild!" Bob was watching the birds with pleasure, the seagulls of the Mediterranean.

"I was in Italy during the war," said the short, skinny, drunken man sitting on the right. "I liked the Mediterranean, too. At one time I stayed in a village; I had lost my way and an Italian peasant family put me up. It was a pleasant village by the seashore. For a week, they took care of me like a king, plenty of butter and honey. For a week they called me 'Sir.' It was 'Sir' all the time. The flavor of that word is still on my palate. You know, no one has said 'sir' to

Three Drunks in the Park

me since then. How could I forget that village? How could I forget that beautiful sea? All the village people showed me respect. I was a stranger to them there, but those people knew the value of a person. At one look they understood who he was. They weren't idiots like us. We couldn't hold a candle to them! The world knows their civilization. What do we have? Nothing! What crap do we have? Just look at our country! Suppose we went to war for this? We risked our lives. Then what? We're miserable, they're comfortable! Damn no-goods! Look at this park, what's it like? Look at those people, all trash.

"I love the Mediterranean, too. Ah, how sweet it is. Man, that's living there! They know the value of a person. With their sweet Italian accent, didn't those people say 'Sir'? I can't describe it. Bob, did anyone ever call you 'Sir'? Bob, call me 'Sir' once! I want to hear it again. Let me taste it again."

"Screw you!" said Bob. "Why should I Sir you, you drunken idiot. Where do you get a Sir, man? As soon as you have a dime, you head for the beer-joint. Is that what Sirs do? Sirs have money! They have class! What have you got? What do you know about the Mediterranean, anyway? Did you learn about the Mediterranean staying in an Italian village?"

"You should have seen and loved the seagulls," said Bob.

"You should have seen the girls," said Al.

Fred was put down, "But, after all, nobody ever called you guys 'Sir,' " he said.

SPRING IN MAGOG

Hard winter began in 1975; a flock of storms, cold, and troubles continued in 1976. The beautiful ground was buried under dirty snow. Like well-water, it stayed below in the depths.

Lines of gray trees, starting at the top of the hill, descend on both sides of the trail all the way to the lake. Summers, their shade is beautiful on this slope. They refresh me. However, in winter they create an emptiness. A gray light dissolves the area.

Silver Light loved this place very much. Two years ago, before she joined her ancestors, she used to say, "I'll always live here. If I do go, my wind will return. I'll take my ancestors' wind and come here." I don't know if she is this wind that's blowing now. The crazy woman always does what she says. She's around here someplace, blowing.

The winter passed in difficulties and troubles. Silver Light was no longer with me. When she was, she used to say a few words that changed my thinking. She was the one among us who was least Indian. She was the fastest in learning changes that came from the city. She quickly adjusted, speaking and thinking as they did. We couldn't conform and remained backward. After Silver Light passed away, we broke up and lived apart in mud and rain.

First she died; Silver Light left us. Then we died; we couldn't pick up and leave so we stayed here, living apart, ruined. Our daughter went to the city, our son became a priest.

This year, Magog encountered a rush of city people bigger than any previous year. They were madly digging for metal everywhere, burrowing nests like moles. We couldn't restrain them. We couldn't do anything but wait it out, like a snowstorm. But it seemed never to end. Silver Light escaped this storm, but then she didn't mind city folks, anyway.

Silver Light brought the spring of 1976. Her wind made all of yesterday's rain. It was she who drove the clouds and brought rain. She shook trees and melted snow with clean rainwater.

Next week, Mary will come from the city. For me, her real name is White Water. Two years ago, after her mother's passing on, she settled in the city. When I saw her short skirts up to her panties and her high cheekbones painted red, I didn't ask where in the city she worked and she didn't say. I closed my ears to what city people said. After all, I'm not from the city. I learned this early in life and don't want to forget it: If a bird is born to a fish, its mother will teach it to swim. But actually, a bird has to fly. So I leave the girl in peace. Let White Water have her city ways, but may her heart remain Indian.

Robert is also coming in a few days, right after the Easter celebration. He'll finally lock up the church and come to see me. My white colt! White Colt grew up and became a priest. Then he became Robert in the city. He's entirely different. "We must remain Indian, we must be close to God," he says.

White Colt has long since forgotten our gods. Just as he's forgotten our free, clean life on the open plains. His heart is citified.

Such thoughts always confuse me. My wife should have been with me. She would have reconciled the two children and brought them to agreement. I'm confused! As far as I'm concerned, they're both on the wrong path. It's as if they both are doing something crooked but I don't know what it is.

The brother and sister easily found work in the city, but their work made them enemies. They had been quarreling for two years. The girl is angry at Robert. I understand the reason for this; Robert knows too but remains silent. So far, I have never heard Robert say anything bad to his sister, but with looks and his not asking her about her job he was making White Water angry.

The two of them have been here three days. Today I understood! It was not only time that had come between us. There was also a silent struggle. Our conversation was short, clipped, and meaningless.

Spring in Magog

No one laughed. There was no enthusiasm. It was as if I were bound to each of them but they were separated from each other. Robert didn't talk, was silent. The girl was depressed and yelled all day. She took a roll of money from her pocket and threw it on the table. "Repair the house!" she said. "If you need more, I'll bring it!"

The crazy wife, as if she were aware of this gray atmosphere, kept blowing around our house. She would strike the tree limbs and make them moan. Like an undisciplined child, she got into everything. This was not the spring wind; I knew it was Silver Light who was blowing. (It's you, isn't it, my snow flower?)

Yesterday, we were looking out the window at the lake. Fall leaves, rotted and chewed under the winter snow, were visible. My daughter was talking about the city. She was telling of the lights, streets, money, and people. She was waiting for one of us to ask her about her job. She wanted to do what she did without secrecy. She wanted to cleanse her citified heart at home.

I didn't have the courage to ask her, because I knew her job and didn't want Robert to be saddened. I felt sorry for the young girl.

I saw the head of an old white rabbit out the window. He was looking timidly from between the trees. One of his long whiskers was wet. This land was his as much as ours. Mary and Robert also saw the rabbit. Silently we watched him from the window.

The rabbit was as timid and fearful as the Indians. He was a stranger in his own woods. Our eyes hurried to follow him. The quarrel between brother and sister suddenly stopped.

The white rabbit approached a little closer to the house. He took a long look at the window. Mary clapped her hands. "Just as it used to be!" she said. "I wonder if this is the same rabbit?"

Our three heads together, we watched the rabbit. Crazy Silver Light shook the trees and house; she wanted to chase the rabbit away. Robert's citified manner disappeared. The hardness in his eyes softened, melted. From underneath, the Indian warmth appeared.

We knew why the rabbit came up to our house. He came to chew the bark of the tree out front. Every year, right at the spring runoff, he came to eat. When he ate the bark, it was considered that spring had come.

Spring in Magog

We watched in excitement. This was our Indian holiday. When we were children, we started celebrating when the rabbit told us spring had come.

Robert and Mary held hands and danced around the chair. The Indian spring had begun. From now on the birds and fish would get fat, their meat sweet. Plenty would come to our tribe, the sunshine would expand over us, the land come to life.

I looked at the children, our winds joined in the same instant. Robert and Mary were no longer citified. We had all become Indian. If was as in the old days again. Above us, Silver Light broke off branches in her joy. The crazy woman was probably drunk.

"Mary," said Robert, "what job do you do in the city?"

Mary laughed. Her high Indian cheekbones broadened.

"I'm a whore!" she said.

CHAMBERPOT MUSIC

Wednesday, a partner in the Quality Teacup Factory, Lebanese Hashem, was looking over the weekly business report. Suddenly his mouth fell open as if he were to say something but couldn't, then he fell flat on his back, unconscious.

Two French workers in the factory's personnel section didn't know what to do. In order to bring Hashem back to consciousness, they dumped two buckets of water on his face. Soaked, Hashem opened his eyes and the words "I'm ruined!" escaped his lips.

The fifty-year-old Lebanese felt exhausted. He didn't want to get up. Wet as he was, he wanted just to lie there. His labors and struggles of so many years had gone up in smoke. He had endured all these difficulties for nothing. His late father used to say, "My son, life is a wet bar of soap; squeeze too hard and it will slip right out of your hand." Hashem used to laugh at such ridiculous remarks.

He looked up to see if he could see God from where he lay, but he saw only the colored ceiling he'd had painted three weeks before. There was no trace of God on the ceiling. Helped by the two French employees, he got up and went inside his office, thinking to himself, "My God, how could they do this to me? What crook changed the settings like that? What will I tell my partners? After all, those two scoundrels have been looking for a way to get rid of me. But I'll work out a solution for this." Yet he couldn't go look. He was afraid of what he would see. Finally, when he did open the door and enter the warehouse, he saw the disaster. There they stood, row upon row. Twenty-two thousand giant teacups . . .

How could he have committed such a blunder? No matter what his partners said, they were right. They had left the factory in his care, in good working order. In just two weeks he had screwed it all up.

Damn these women. When a fifty-year-old guy runs off to Miami like a green kid chasing eighteen-year-old babes, this is what happens. The two weeks he had spent on the seashore under a blazing sun were now completely unbearable. While slowly turning about, he simultaneously appraised the disastrous gigantic teacups and thought about the cause of the disaster. Oh, those hips, wow! Those French girls' hips, fresh as lettuce, they were something else! Hashem smiled. When they're popping fresh, grapes are good to eat.

Hashem was devastated over the scene before him. The place was filled with giant teacups. During those two weeks he'd spent in Miami, the calibration on the machine that made the teacups slipped out of order, and out had come thick teacups as big as middle-sized jugs. The company would suffer tens of thousands of dollars' loss. Hashem picked up one of the enormous teacups and examined it carefully. "I'm bankrupt!" he moaned. The cups had been made of the finest expensive porcelain. He threw the cup on the floor, saying, "Damn it all! For the sake of two weeks' pleasure, I filled with horsecrap the well it took me ten years to dig with a needle. Oh, stupid Hashem, you've ruined yourself! How did this scandalous thing happen? Who messed up the setting on the machine? Have you ever seen such bad luck? Hashem, Hashem! You're not the owner any longer. You're ruined! You've been completely ruined! You'll be lucky if your plump wife at home doesn't kick you in the rump and throw you out."

He wrapped one of the enormous teacups, put it under his arm, closed the factory early, and headed for home. What could he do with a teacup this big?

His house was like a public bath with the water cut off. It was all disorganized. The smell of food wafted from the kitchen, everywhere. The grandchildren were still yelling. When he opened the door, his nose encountered a fragrant aroma. The smell of onions and frying fish spread outside. This smell comforted Hashem somewhat. His nerves relaxed. He was home at last. Hashem's buxom wife took the package from him at the door.

Chamberpot Music

"Oh, thanks, honey!" she said. "So you brought me a present from Miami? Thanks again! I was unhappy when you went, but you really know how to please a person."

Hashem, already overwhelmed with trouble, hadn't the strength to reply. A sound like "huuuh!" slipped between his teeth.

Upon opening the package, she howled, "Are you making fun of me? You've brought me a chamberpot and you're not even embarrassed? Now, what am I going to do with a chamberpot? I should break it over your head! Just don't think that I didn't know about your fooling around with those filthy women in Miami. I'm quiet only to avoid breaking these poor kids' hearts. You always do something to demean me."

Hashem looked sadly at his wife. "By God! Madam, this isn't a chamberpot," she replied, "it's a teacup."

When the woman heard these words, she screamed again. "Don't you see, you're still making sport with me? What is there about this that's a teacup? There's no teacup this big!"

Hashem: "By God, this is a teacup!"

Hashem's older daughter, Ayshe, came into the room. She looked at the enormous teacup in her mother's hands. "Papa, this is just an ordinary chamberpot," she said, "and a nice one at that." Then she called out, "Farid, come here, son!"

Little Farid appeared from the adjacent room, bare-bottomed, a chocolate in his hand. Ayshe put Farid on the potty. "Sit there and grunt, my boy!" He hadn't been able to go for three days. His bowels were bound. He grunted and first the sound of pee was heard, then something fell into the water, "plop!" Glowing, Hashem smiled with affection. Ayshe asked, "Father, where did you find this lovely chamberpot? Did you see how quickly his bowels loosened up?"

In his mind, Hashem was toying with a number of ideas. He didn't answer his daughter; instead, grabbing his hat, he rushed out.

Hashem took ten of the pots he had on hand to a friend who sold porcelain and left them on consignment at his shop. The next day, he dropped by the shop and watched the buyers come and go. He observed them looking with excitement at the chamberpots. On the third day, half of the ten pots had been sold. Hashem had just

Chamberpot Music

one thing in mind. Then, on the fourth day, he approached a middle-aged, scrawny man who had bought a chamberpot.

"We're making a marketing survey of our factory's products. I would like to ask you a few questions. In return for your help, we'll make you a gift of this chamberpot you purchased. Why did you buy it?"

"I'll tell you why I bought this chamberpot, but you're not to laugh at me. You must not make fun of me and I don't want my name to appear in the newspaper."

"Don't worry, we'll keep your name secret."

The man looked furtively about him, then he softly explained: "You know, the chamberpot, right! Don't laugh, but it reminds me of my mother. When I sit down on one, I close my eyes and bring back my childhood. I become a baby. In that moment, the troubles and struggles of the whole day are over. Like a drunk, I lose myself. My mother appears in my mind. She takes my hand. 'My son!' she says and hugs and kisses me. So it is then that I forget the mistreatment and insulting remarks I've received at the office. Worries about my low pay and the high cost of living disappear. It seems like a joke to you, doesn't it? Well, just ask me more about this pleasure. As soon as I pull down my trousers and sit on the chamberpot, another world awaits me. The city life, so wearing to my nerves, disappears. On the chamberpot, I'm as cool as a fresh cucumber. The squabbles of my crazy children cease to exist. I hear music in my ears. Just look at this ugly life. You call this living? Corpses await their turns at the cemetery gates. There are strikes like fires burning everywhere. All the mothers have left their children and chase after jobs. Children *need* a chamberpot, but no one sees this. Thank you; whoever brought this chamberpot out on the market has saved us all."

Hashem listened with enthusiasm. Following are notes collected from his daily questionnaires:

"The chamberpot transmits a feeling of nearness between mothers, fathers, and children. The potty insures a closeness between a child and his mother. A child who squats on a potty in a warm, pleasant corner will grow up healthy. In modern life, a child's mother

Chamberpot Music

and father are not together enough. Children of this generation are growing up distrustful. As babies, they never got enough babyhood."

When Hashem looked over the report again, he was delighted, overjoyed. Half of his problem had been solved. He had finally found a good market for his product. He was sure all the chamberpots he had on hand would be sold if he opened a well-planned marketing campaign.

With the consent of his two partners, a campaign for the sale of chamberpots was opened on television with a one-and-a-half-minute commercial each morning and evening. Scenes of sleeping or playing children accompanied by lullaby music comprised the broadcast. Finally the sweet smile of a child sitting on the potty appeared. A woman with her head screened by mist was the mother. A mother's touch in the ad signified the boundless trust a chamberpot brought to a person's life.

The busy American society, rushing to and from work, paid scant attention to this vacuous commercial for the first few weeks, but on the third weekend, things began to change. Slowly, the chamberpots began to sell.

As the demand for the three-dollar chamberpots increased, Hashem raised the price. As advertising on television and radio increased, sales also grew. At the end of the seventh week, all the chamberpots on hand had been sold. But the demand that followed hadn't been satisfied.

The three partners put their heads together and debated what they should do in face of the continuing demand. They changed the teacup factory into one that produced chamberpots.

In six months, the demand, which originated in six cities, spread over all America. The factory now produced chamberpots day and night in an effort to keep up with sales.

According to research Hashem conducted, each evening between the hours of nine and ten, in order to forget the trials and tribulations of the day and enjoy the warmth and trust of a mother's embrace, all America was sitting on chamberpots. At nine each evening, entire families took out their chamberpots, turned on their radios, and relaxed to the melodies of classical music. This mode of relaxation spread throughout America. At the end of the ninth month, the estimable Mr. Hashem had put nine modern factories into the service of the nation.

The marvelous chamberpots of the Quality Teacup Factories in a short time enveloped all America and became a part of society that could never be abandoned.

In all the cities of the New World, Thanksgiving celebrations were organized to honor Mr. Hashem, who had made all this happiness possible for them.

SNIFFLES REJEP

I could never get rid of my cold. Sniffling and sneezing exhausted and made me hoarse. I couldn't talk. If I opened my mouth, an odd wheezing came from my throat. It's not easy to sneeze seven times a minute. It would even ruin a trumpet. That's life! Overdo just once and you're through.

If it had been only my voice getting hoarse from sneezing, OK, but when a person starts getting troubles, they come by the ton. At every sneeze, the inside of my head shook as if in an earthquake. These quakes shook my eyes from their sockets. One of my pupils slipped to the left, the other to the right. I couldn't see straight. How could my eyes endure such violence? My poor pupils swam around in the void like single beans in soup. When people looked at me, first they said, "Oh, the poor fellow!" Then they laughed at my condition. Why shouldn't they laugh? This type of lopsided defect hasn't even been written up in the medical journals yet. As far as I know, cross-eyed people's eyes are off by a known angle, the degree of this angle staying the same. If the left eye slips to the right, it stays that way. As for my cross-eyes, they're like a shack built by a railroad track: my eyes slip a little every time I sneeze, just as the shack moves a few centimeters every time the train goes by.

It wouldn't be so bad if it had been only my voice and eyes that were affected. I would have accepted that gratefully. But if a person's head shakes every second like an autumn leaf, the vertebrae in his neck become slack. My neck was all loose.

When I breathed, my head swayed back and forth like a street light caught by the wind. If I didn't grasp my head in my hands and hold it, it would never stop swinging.

Sniffles Rejep

In a person's life, troubles come in strings like the unraveling of a knitted stocking. This sickness made my ears run. I couldn't hear well. I was an embarrassment to the whole neighborhood. If only I could get rid of my cold, perhaps all these troubles would come to an end.

The mucous stuck in my nose like glue. It didn't want to leave its comfortable warm place. Damn the fall! Summer sniffles, winter sniffles. Spring sniffles, autumn sniffles. I couldn't talk for sneezing. If you sneeze after each syllable, who can understand what you say, anyway? If only this had been the sum of my troubles! Sometimes the sneezing caused a lapse of memory. May it never happen to you! Just as I started on a subject, "Hatchoo!" The subject I was talking about flew from my head like a bird. Then I looked at the faces of my listeners and tried to figure out what we'd been talking about. OK, find a new subject! I continued talking as if nothing had changed. If it fit, fine! If not, a crying shame!

Summer came. "Thank God, I'll finally get rid of this dirty cold," I say. Fat chance! Just like the cold weather and storms, my cold hung on. Then I want to go out and enjoy the sun and warmth like everyone else. But no use! "Hatchoo, hatchoo!" I'm a radio with static. While some people undress and refresh themselves at the rivers and lakes, and some drink iced drinks and smoke fragrant cigarettes, I flap my wings like a wounded chicken and sneeze. I drag myself around with a big fat red nose, a quaking head, cross-eyes, and a stuttering voice.

"See here," I tell my wife, "this isn't very reasonable; people catch colds for a week, two weeks or at the most a month. Mine last for months, for seasons. I don't know whether to go to the doctor or what."

"Forget it," my wife said, "you've always had a cold. After all, when did you ever have good health? You were always sniffly, and weren't you the one whose voice always went 'Ahem, ahem!' and who was known at school as Sniffles Rejep? Just tell me now!"

My wife was right. I had been sniffly since way back. She said, "I'm not complaining, so why are you carrying on? You're making a mountain out of a molehill all by yourself. Aren't there aspirin and Kleenex in the house? When your nose runs, use the Kleenex;

Sniffles Rejep

if you have a cold, take aspirin when you go to bed; you'll get up in the morning feeling fine."

I mustn't treat this sensitive woman unjustly. She was showing me more concern than she'd ever done before. She knew more about my health than I did.

First she filled the house with Kleenex. "Don't worry, Mister," she said, "the next time you have the sniffles, I'll have twenty boxes of Kleenex for you." "What in the devil kind of a cold is this?" I say. "It's two days since I got rid of it but my nose is still like an eggplant and I don't want to catch another cold!" But just as if I hadn't been the one who said this, the next day, again, "Hatchoo! Hatchoo!"

They say women are sensitive. Well, my woman is more sensitive than any. Like a weather-forecasting station, she knows in a flash on what day and when I'll catch a cold. She filled the inside of the house with Kleenex. Whatever drawer or closet I opened, it was crammed full with Kleenex. Understandably, much of the kitchen money went for this. I couldn't say anything. If I opened my mouth, I would just get myself in trouble. She would say, "You use all the medicated handkerchiefs. Then, without shame, you complain, don't you?" Therefore, I keep my mouth shut for now.

Our budget's in trouble. We have long since lost the TV and the dining and living room sets that we bought on time. We couldn't make the payments because of the great increase in kitchen expenses. One morning, showing us no pity, the repossessors loaded everything on a truck and took it away. The house remained completely bare. Within a week, my wife had filled the empty closets with Kleenex.

While the Kleenex boxes increased in number, as though having a cold were a stipulation, our little daughter started checking, first thing in the morning, to see if I had one. "Papa, do you have a cold today?" she asked. "Daughter," I replied, "do you have bad intentions toward me?" She chuckled up her sleeve. Her mother broke in. "Why are you cross with the child? As if there's a day when you don't have a cold! She only asks because she loves you."

A cold is terrible. For no reason, I lose everything. At night, I carefully roll up and put on a chair my overcoat, scarf, socks, shirt, and sweater, because I go to work early in the morning. I hate to hunt all over, when I awaken, for my socks and sweater.

But no matter what I do, everything goes wrong. My clothes started disappearing together with the winter months. In the morning, I look and I have no socks. Well! Last night I put them here with my own hands. What happened to the bastards? After all, fairies and goblins didn't steal them during the night! Want to or not, I go to work sockless. Are you the one who went out without socks? In the evening, I return home sniffling and sneezing. My daughter is laughing up her sleeve. My wife says, "So, dear hubby, you have a cold again?" It's as if when I get a cold she behaves nicer and sweeter toward me. When it seems I'm getting rid of my cold, my wife frowns and her voice hardens. On some days, I actually search for a cold, but God, never once, went along with this wish of mine.

Not only my socks disappeared, you'd think the flea market merchants also took off my pants and jacket.

One morning, as if they had been spying on me when I washed my hair the night before, I saw that my hat had vanished. It seemed as though someone would celebrate if I died from catching cold. If I told my wife, she would say, "You didn't take care of your things when you were young, either. How many times did you lose your watch or fountain pen? So now it's your hat. Your things have the habit of getting lost!"

What kind of logic is that? Can things lose themselves?

Finally, I became experienced in this business. I knew that if I washed my hair in the evening, I would lose my hat in the morning. Therefore, I went to bed with the hat tied to my leg. What a pity, this didn't work, either.

When I got up one morning, my hat had vanished. Someone had cut the string with scissors. That's how it was that I couldn't get rid of colds for a whole year due to hats, socks, and sweaters.

No matter how much I praise my wife to the skies, it's truly too little. I wrongfully accused the woman. I thought it was she who was hiding my socks, shirts, and hat so that I would catch a cold. It also crossed my mind that she wanted to kill me and marry someone else. Then I looked at her and said, "Hey, what bastard other than me would that face attract?" If someone told me, "You're no better than she is, *wrinklepuss!*" they'd be right. "Look at your nose! It's not a nose, it's a rearing camel's hump! There's a wet red mountain sitting in the middle of your face!"

Today, once again, my wife proved the love she has for me. "Mister!" she said (it had been a long time since I had heard this word from her sweet lips). "You can never get rid of your cold living this way. Let's buy Kleenex wholesale instead of retail and reduce our expenses." What a bright idea! "Right on!" I said. "Whenever you want, let's buy them." My wife had even figured the price. A half truckload of Kleenex, $2,500.

She was going to make a total investment of two thousand five hundred dollars. "Madam, have you lost your mind?" I said. "Where are we going to find this kind of money?" She replied, "And I thought you were a businessman. Sell your antique watch! Let's buy Kleenex! We'll make a profit of two thousand five hundred dollars." I replied, "Well, I had never thought of that."

The antique watch was let go and the house filled with Kleenex. "Don't you see?" my wife explained. "We've now been saved from medical expenses. Use these paper handkerchiefs in place of bath and hand towels. We'll save on laundry and soap and hot water, too! Most important, there'll be more time to spend with you. Just think, the two of us together, like old times."

I was going to say, "Since all the furniture's gone, where are we going to sit and talk, Madam?" but I changed my mind. It was nice that she thought of that, really. She was enduring all this trouble because of me. After all, I was the one who had the cold; she wasn't.

My wife said, "These paper handkerchiefs will bring you good luck. You'll see, your cold will be over and you'll no longer lose your things. You won't cough and sniffle as you used to." She was right in this. As soon as the house was filled with Kleenex, the hats, socks, and sweaters I had lost returned. Windows that had come open by themselves, even though I had closed them securely at night, now remained closed. It was as if an "orderliness fairy" had come to our house. Everything began to run like clockwork.

My wife and daughter sang all day. Everything was shiny clean. Meals were prepared with delight and eaten in peace. "My dear husband," she said, my sweet-tempered wife, "because of your gener-

Sniffles Rejep

osity, I saved two hours today. I didn't launder towels or bathrobes. There's no more need for kitchen towels. We have Kleenex for everything. On top of that, we're saving money."

If it hasn't happened to you, you couldn't know. How many days was it that my wife said, "I don't wash the towels anymore," and I passed it off with, "That's nice!" Finally, while I was taking my evening shower, it dawned on me what she meant. There were no towels in the bathroom. I asked my wife for a towel and she said, "What do you want with a towel? Dry yourself with Kleenex!" I used two boxes of Kleenex, at seventy cents a box, one dollar and forty cents! "Madam, this Kleenex business will sink us, make us beggars. Let's give back the boxes still left," I insisted. "My cold is better, anyway. I won't ever get a cold again."

But did she listen to me? No, she closed her eyes and opened her mouth. "Have you seen such a selfish husband? When he has a cold, he doesn't say a word. I didn't expect this of you. I regret all those years I devoted to you. You're talking about two or three dollars' worth of paper. Because of this paper I've had a little time to spend with my beloved husband, but naturally he doesn't care."

In six months we exhausted all the Kleenex. Two thousand five hundred dollars down the drain. All the house furnishings lost. Money in the bank gone. We're poor as church mice.

When my wife saw my unhappy brooding—it must have been to console me—she said, "I wanted to help out. Soon we'll be rich. We'll be well known in this country. Everyone will greet you, saying, 'There's Mr. Rejep!' You'll no longer be Rejep the Immigrant. The hard days are finally over. What were the old days? When the sun came up, instead of making everything bright, it darkened my heart. Very soon, the golden days will appear. Come on, kiss your wife! If it were up to you, we'd remain snot-nosed immigrants. If you hadn't had a smart wife, you would have run from pillar to post like a dog."

She spoke with conviction and sincerity. I was about to be led astray myself. "Madam, what happened? Did we win the lottery? Tell me!" The woman's eyes were sparkling. "What good's a lottery? You're going to be a well-known man, Rejep! Rejep, my lion!" Even though it was a lie, my ego began to puff up when I heard those words. "Wait!" she said. "Soon, very soon."

Saturday night, you'd think our house was the county fair. My wife had borrowed the neighbor's TV for one day to watch a program. The house smelled of cookies and turnovers. It wasn't a holiday or an outing, so why all the celebration? She had brought two chairs from the other neighbor and since morning had been pouring out orders, "Hurry, eat your food! Don't touch anything! Take your shower early! Dress up!" Lots of other remarks without rhyme or reason. I was going out. "No!" she said. "Stay at home!"

At eight o'clock we lined up in front of the television. First they showed a soft furry rabbit on the screen, then swans swimming on the water. "More commercials!" I told my wife. "This is a Kleenex commercial, too." My wife's eyes shone. "Turn it off, Madam!" I said. "It was this Kleenex that ruined us. So why do we watch their ads?" "Leave it on!" she said.

On the screen, an announcer started talking: "Dear listeners! As you know, the Kleenex factories, who are always thinking of the good of our public, opened a paper-handkerchief-consumption contest. A hundred boxes of Kleenex will be given the family who consumed the most this year. In addition, they will be presented a plaque of honor. It will be arranged for this family to tour our factory and be presented to our General Director. Furthermore, two lucky winners will receive valuable gifts in a drawing; the first-prize winner will be paid one hundred thousand dollars, the second-prize winner will receive a week-long tour of Europe with all expenses paid by our factory."

I listened to the speaker with an amazed look on my face. My wife was speechless with excitement. The announcer continued, "Now bring out the coupons you have been collecting the past year. The drawing will be held within two minutes."

Just then my wife came back with two big boxes. "What's this?" I asked her.

"Kleenex coupons!" she said.

WEATHER SCIENCE

Who says that immigrants will all be left high and dry in this country? Whoever says so is crazy; they're communists and fascists! Is there a better immigrant than I am? I have everything you need to be an immigrant. My face is rather ugly. I have a large nose. My skin is close to being swarthy. I speak halting, broken English. I know a foreign language. If you see me in the street, I don't have to tell you—you'll say, "Aha, here comes another immigrant," and beat a retreat. I'm clumsy. I smell of onions; I eat lots of them. You can't be much more of an immigrant than that!

My being an immigrant didn't prevent me from becoming Assistant General Director. I'm now a happy man. I consider myself as happy as a native son. I lack for nothing, thank God. Really, they know my value where I work. They don't contradict what I say. I have a very important job helping Canadian workers do their work without discomfort and with relief. It is our job to provide that relief when they are in great need. We perform this function at remote construction sites, bridges, harbors, and airports where we rent portable toilets.

Just don't think that renting portable johns is an easy job. You have to figure how many people work at the site, what the workers eat, what they drink, and how many times a day they use the biffy. Lack of comfortable access to toilets for workers has a negative effect on the developing economy. It opens the door for delays in the completion of projects, and production falls. This job requires delicate accounting, and it wasn't easy for me to advance in it. However, no one hindered me because of my being an immigrant.

Now, as I look out the window, I recall those first exciting weeks of my immigration to Canada. Though many years have passed, I can never forget my arrival in April. A gangling youth, I landed at Winnipeg airport that bright spring morning like a chirping bird. Half the world was mine; the other half belonged to Gabriel from Mersin, who greeted me.

That year, those spring months passed like a dream. The days seemed colorful, cloudy gray, confused, meaninglessly empty, or pleasant to me. With every passing day I observed new facets of the life-styles around me. That's why some days were empty, some confused, and some meaningful and colorful. When we met at the airport, Gabriel had said, "You'll be dazed for a day or two but don't worry! It's the change in time. In a week you'll be OK." Actually, I was befuddled for ten whole years.

I looked about me with blank eyes, like Hasan Hüseyin looking at unreadable Chinese writing. Here was an ideal city, an ideal life on this country plain. What a pleasant place! A city like a pie on a tray. Cut it up and eat it! God picked up His cleaver and cut everyone a piece. As for the sky, it glowed above us like a dusty mirror. The streets of this plains city extended as far as the eye could see, all decorated with flowers, trees, children, and young girls. It was an enormous park. People didn't live here, it was a society of fairies. I saw no one frowning. An inexhaustible holiday atmosphere blew everywhere.

The week I arrived, Gabriel gave me a good talking to. "Listen, stupid," he said, "these straight, hard-working people are fed up with empty talk. Stay away from subjects like poetry, music, philosophy, and politics or they'll mock you. Look around you! Is anyone involved with poetry or philosophy? They work like ants. Do you see any shirkers? There's a way, a system to every job. That's how you live here!"

I listened to Gabriel with equanimity, like a cow eating grass. Gabriel had changed. He was a curse. If I sneezed, "You sneezed wrong," he would say. "Gabriel, is there a system for sneezing? If you sneeze, you just sneeze! There's no right or wrong about it. Gee, even if I am a foreigner, I'm not the only blockhead around here." Not even that shut Gabriel up. He chewed me out, saying, "Your sneeze was very rude, noisy, like a thunderbolt. You must sneeze more courteously."

Weather Science

I caught a cold, a bad one, and had not only a high fever but also a runny nose. I was sick, wiped out, but Gabriel still carried on. "What kind of a cold is that? What a clumsy way to spread a cold! You infected your face with your hands! You ruin everything! You're driving me crazy!" he said.

"Gabriel, have the kindness to realize that a nose is like that! It won't stop running when you want. Whose nose would stop like a trained dog when you say 'Stop!' or run when you say 'Run'? Only it knows when to run. How am I going to get my nose to listen to me?"

There was no evil in Gabriel's heart. I know he wanted to help me. In this foreign place, he wanted me to be respected and make lots of money.

I realized it wouldn't work out. My ideas put him in a bad mood; whatever I did went wrong. Following this way of life in this great country, I would stay hungry. That son-of-a-gun, Gabriel, would stand me in front of him, close his eyes, open his mouth, then pin my ears back, saying, "Don't do this, don't do that, this is the way things are!"

"Enough!" I said. "This business has got to stop right here. Friend, I'll herd this camel better by myself!" I started to carefully observe the Canadians, taking notes on the spot of everything they said. Then, in the evening, when I examined my notes, the thing that struck me was the two points they knew very well. First, they knew the subject of the job they worked on; second, they talked incessantly about the weather. Everyone I knew was a specialist on one thing. Car salesman Dan sold only red automobiles. With his eyes closed, he could tell from the sound of a passing car the make, model, and color. If he listened to the motor, he could tell where and what kind of trouble there was in an instant. Accountant Ralph could tell at a glance if my multiplication was right or wrong. He never made a mistake in figures. Doctor Tom noticed from a woman's walk whether or not she was pregnant. Bachelor Harvey could tell from the look in a girl's eyes whether or not anything was doing. Cross-eyed Jerry was a housepainter. He painted walls better than anyone. Stuttering Watson smiled between syllables to fill the gaps.

I was amazed at Canadians' knowledge of their work. In addition, everyone was a weather forecaster. They knew minute by minute when it would rain, hail, or snow. They dressed accordingly and

Weather Science

their conversations were always about the weather. They discussed it with pleasure, seeking and learning the most interesting aspects of the subject.

Just don't think that small talk is easy. If a person doesn't know well what he's talking about, he can mess himself up. To talk about the weather, one must first know the kinds and names of clouds and how they are formed. He has to know if rain, snow, or hail falls from white, black, or gray clouds. All my friends knew everything about this. It's also necessary to learn the names of the winds and their velocities. If you don't know which clouds come with which winds, you're in trouble.

In order to study these subjects, I enrolled in the university. For three years I learned the states of the weather and wind. During the second three years, I made a study in depth on the subjects of snow, rain, and storms, Enjoying my research, I broadened my field. In six years I received my diploma, then, studying an additional year, I received my doctorate. When I finished the university, there was no one in my circle who knew as much as I did about the weather and portable toilets.

After I had memorized the names of three hundred twenty kinds of human excrement, I needed only to be asked and I could tell you from whom it came and his job qualifications. I wrote two books on this subject. Thank God, I have received recognition for my labors. I have met with respect and affection. My knowledge, experience, and horizons have broadened. Now I look upon crazy, nonsensical subjects with contempt.

Last year, I represented Canada at the United Nations. You should have seen me then! I solved even the most complicated problems easily. The speeches I gave on weather, wind, precipitation, snow, and storms were talked about for days. From then on, my name was known everywhere. National problems were not decided without consulting me.

Such important questions as the land situation in central Canada; American-Russian relations on foodstuffs; the question of finding a place for disposal of human excrement, which was multiplying dangerously day by day; the effect of the weather situation on world production of wheat; whether or not a sewer system was necessary for excess world rainfall—all such questions were subjects that could not be solved without consulting me.

I can certainly be considered a fortunate man.

PALEFACE

The old man sat in a copper-embossed chair and explained:

Life wasn't like this long ago; it used to have ups and downs. Some years were good, some bad. People, on the one hand, and Nature, on the other, brought changes into daily life. Some seasons, there was too much rain and floods came. Others, there was drought, with hunger and want.

Also, there was a curse of God, something they called "Fashion." Every year you changed what you wore. Whether it was new or old, it was shameful to wear something you had worn the year before. Then, too, making children was another worry. It took a lot of effort and you were never sure of the result. If you wanted a girl, the woman gave birth to a boy. You expected a boy and the baby was a girl. While you expected one, sometimes twins or triplets sprouted. What an unplanned, disorganized life!

In those days I was a poor person. Naturally, *you* don't know what a wealthy or poor person is. How should I explain? Well, look at it this way: some people had lots of everything and others had nothing at all. Then some people had material things but others had none. What I'm trying to say is that life was confusing.

In those days, Nature sought out the poor and oppressed them. Any troubles and curses she had to give, went to the poor. I don't know why she took sides. Maybe she didn't take sides but just found it convenient to do it that way. It seemed there was no one else on earth but the poor for her to give a bad time to. Intentional injustice and rudeness! But what could I do? If the one giving me a bad time was the judge, whom could I tell my troubles to?

Though all these wealthy creatures existed on earth, Nature found me to drown in trouble. In those days, the world was a different place. Everything was measured with money. Some earned little money, others much. Hard work brought in little money; those who worked little earned a lot.

"Gentlemen, please, I beg of you, let me work little and pay me much!" I pleaded.

"Impossible!" they answered.

"Look, my people at home are hungry, miserable. Just grant me a little more of that poison called money so I can work with peace of mind."

No one listened. Meanwhile, my neighbor was swimming in wealth. He lacked for nothing. Money flowed for him like a millstream.

"I don't want it!" he used to yell.

"Impossible!" they replied. "We'll force you to take it. Otherwise, the charm on this job will be broken. If a cog slips just once, we're ruined!"

"Very well, when will I become like my neighbor?" I asked one day.

"You'll never be like him," they answered. "You're not one of Them."

Come on, who were the ones you call Them? They were They. They were different. My head ached from all the asking, a headache aspirin wouldn't cure.

Thank God, those days are past and gone. We were saved! We have now arrived at this great system. I recall days past very well. I was pathetic and destitute. My wife was pregnant every year. When I said, "My gosh, how does it happen? Why don't *all* wives get pregnant each year?" some scoundrel answered, "Because of your naked poverty, that's why!"

Children flowed into the house like leaves from the calendar. First we filled the rooms with children, then the halls. Soon there'd be no room left for us. Whatever room or drawer you opened, out would pop a child. Further, as if Nature wanted to be stubborn, she gave us children whose appetites couldn't be satisfied. Whenever I took one on my lap, with closed eyes and open mouth the baby would beg for food. Others' babies were not like that. They had to be coaxed to eat. When they wouldn't, the doctor was immediately called. I got so angry at those pink-skinned, fat babies. If you looked

Paleface

at my kids, they were like hungry wolves. If they got their hands on it, they'd even chew on wood. Ours seemed to be born with teeth.

As if so many children weren't enough, that year we had twins. Good Lord Almighty! with the money I made, I had to leave my family half-starved. Furthermore, it wasn't as easy to fix meals as it is now. You bought food at the market and cooked it at home. To provide the energy you get from today's food you had to eat tons of that. Inflation also lurked, a problem that was not to be endured. I told Nature, "Come on, now, if you're going to give too much of something, can't you think of something besides children? You're unmerciful!"

We had suffered a lot even before the first child was born. My wife is a frail skinny woman. Due to working her fingers to the bone, she couldn't find time to gain weight. Come on, merciless Nature, how did you crowd twins into this woman's belly? With so many fat women existing on earth, why did you keep searching until you found her? Was it deliberate? My wife's skin is paper-thin from lack of nourishment. We check every day to see if it's cracking. Her stomach has expanded like a balloon. We expect it to explode any day. I really can't understand the hurry. Couldn't she have babies one by one? There's no gain, only hard work.

One day, lost in hopelessness, I went to the place where I work. "Give me a job that pays a lot of money!" I said.

"Impossible! You're not one of Them," they replied.

This time I really got mad. "I'd like to see one of those creatures you call Them. How are they different from me? Are their ears long, their noses short?"

Someone said, "They have two belly buttons!" Someone else, "They have pale faces." Actually, the people they described didn't seem human. Like print dresses washed in hot water, their colors had faded. Their eyes were all dirty blue or green. "Come on, what's the difference between them and me?" I asked, but no one knew. How had these low-down people bleached themselves like this? That I had to learn.

One day I captured one of these paleface people and took him home. If I couldn't learn their secret, I would die. All of us would

Paleface

die of hunger. I told this paleface I had captured, "Undress! Undress now so I can see you! Let's see where you're different from us!"

Then I called my wife. "Come and see," I said. Upon seeing my wife, the paleface said, "I won't undress!"

"Look here, undress or I'll cut you up!"

In fear, the paleface immediately stripped. Darned if the creature I'd captured as a man didn't turn out to be a woman! My aim wasn't to see the body of a paleface naked; I just wanted to see how they differed from me.

When the woman appeared stark naked, I told my wife, "Madam, look this woman over and let's see how she differs from you." The paleface creature screamed and yelled. "Come on," I said, "we're not going to harm you. Quiet! We have no bad intentions!" but she wouldn't listen.

My wife examined the woman very carefully all over. "I can't see any difference," she said.

"Impossible, that's impossible. They must be different from us!" I asked the woman, "What do you have more of than us?" The detestable woman replied, "Brains!" I was going to give her the back of my hand but thought better of it. I told my wife, "You've upset the applecart. Now take a good look and discover the difference." My wife, with her great belly, insisted, "Nothing's different!"

"For heaven's sake, take a *good* look. Check everywhere. These cursed creatures hide their differences so we can't learn about them. You can't trust them. If we can't find how they differ, we'll pass out of this world in hunger. Look at yourself. You're like a drum. God only knows how many children fill your belly. We have neither enough food nor enough money. They are exploiting us. Look carefully, don't miss a thing! Look like a detective searching for a clue. Now look at that spot. Feel it to see if it's dirt or a mole. I didn't notice those three moles on top of her leg. Wet your finger and rub them. Will they come off? The low-down creatures! They came off, didn't they? So they weren't real moles. Don't I know these palefaces? They could steal the gold from your teeth."

My wife inspected the naked woman standing before us like a plucked chicken bought from the market. She checked her over from head to toe to see if she had something attached.

Finally, the woman began to feel sorry for us and tried to help us find the difference. "If you'd like," she said, "let's start all over again. Let's compare everything, one by one. Only in that way can we discover any excesses or shortages."

"OK!" I agreed, "a good idea. God bless you. See, Madam, these palefaces have good hearts inside."

While the two women were comparing their bodies, they discovered that the paleface woman had a scar on her body below her navel. In excitement, the two of them cried, "We've found it! It must be this scar."

"Let me look!" I said. A rather wide scar from an operation. "What's this?" I asked the woman.

"I don't know."

"Did you have this scar when you were born?"

"No," the poor woman replied.

"OK then!" I said. "They change people to palefaces with this operation. But we have to learn what they take out or put in."

The naked woman grinned from ear to ear. "Do you think they changed my color through there?"

ANYONE WANT A MILLION DOLLARS?

The man who told me this tale was thin and tall. He quietly sipped on his beer and talked as if mocking his listeners. It was obvious from his accent that he was European:

When I won the biggest lottery of the year, I sprouted wings and flew for joy. Like a crazy chicken I was suddenly free; there were no obstacles in my path, no limits, no restrictions. Finally, everything was mine! A million dollars is easy to say, but it turned my world upside down. Just think a minute; are you ready for it? Suddenly, they throw you into the middle of a million greenbacks. If you want to go on a trip, like choosing a melon at the market, you can pick any country you want. If you want a house, an apartment, a mansion, or a castle, everything's yours! "The battle's over, friends," I said, "peace was declared yesterday! Political quarrels are over! Who wants to fight over big international appointments? Not me! I just want to live my life quietly, comfortably."

When I won the lottery, I learned just how many friends I had and my chest swelled with pride. Bless them! They outdid each other in trying to protect my winnings from harm.

My banker friend said, "First you have to change the geography of your face. If you carry on your life with that map, your capital will go down the drain in three days. Just look at your physiognomy. I don't like the looks of it: two small eyes, a great nose, and ears one can't tell from a leaf or fan. That's no face, it's a mountainous region that's suffered an earthquake. Everything's exaggerated, all messed up. Now, don't be offended! I'm saying this for your own good. They'll give you no rest with that face and head. You better change both of them."

Anyone Want a Million Dollars?

"For hell sakes!" I exploded. "What's with you? A man can't change his appearance for no reason. My wife would divorce me! As a matter of fact, she's been spoiling for a fight. How could I go out among people with a new face? What harm does my empty, meaningless face do you? Get off my back!"

My doctor friend told me, "Chum, your eyes are like looking through wide-open windows with no curtains. They reveal the emptiness inside. One look into your eyes and it's instantly apparent that your head is completely vacant. It becomes obvious from your conversation that you're without ideas, understanding, or experience. Even your walk is funny. You walk like a monkey with his arms swinging from side to side. Everything about you shows you're not one of *us*. To become one of *us*, you have to think and live as *we* do. If you don't change, you'll die like a fish out of water. Your head isn't compatible with your money. Until yesterday, you were one of *them*, addlepated, gluttonous, and greedy. Now you need a new outlook, new logic, and new knowledge, just as you need new clothes!"

My other banker told me, "If you don't change that head, by God, the money will fly from your hands. A million dollars has a mind of its own, its own feelings. Will that poor little million stay with a person who can't protect it? I'm surprised at your lack of intelligence. A million dollars flows to the one who loves it. It flows without your even being aware of it. It goes day or night, but it goes. You must change!"

Another doctor friend: "If you don't conform to your new life, your body won't last long, you'll die. You'll have to eliminate sugars and fats! From now on you won't be able to eat everything you want. You must watch your diet. Every year, you should have a heart, stomach, and bowel examination. Also, you must participate in a little sport every day. No more laziness! Eat little, eat carefully!" he warned.

Have you ever heard of such a business? What's happened to me? I can't eat or drink. From now on, I'm forbidden foods with the onions that I love so much. It's not respectable to eat food with garlic. I've lost the good life, it's ruined. If you only knew what I've put up with. There aren't words to tell you. The wife of our engineer neighbor said, "Gee, are you going to stay married to that bandy-legged woman? How can you go out in society with that slouch? Everyone will boo you. Come, listen to me, let's find you a woman fit for a millionaire, a lady who looks like one, a proper wife."

My reporter friend advised, "Expect a big disaster. Even a five-year-old girl of the new generation knows how to take your money, like picking tomatoes off the vine, and you wouldn't even know it! Change, renew yourself!"

But the priest really scared me. "Renew your faith in God!" he said. "Study people! Learn the difference between the lazy and the industrious, the consumer and the producer! Let no one snatch away your wealth! Deprive not the poor of their poverty! Realize that you were created to do something useful with your money for those devoted to God!"

I was greatly alarmed, could neither eat nor drink, couldn't sleep nights, even had trouble walking. Sometimes when both my right and left leg wanted to step forward at the same time, I fell flat on my face. A time or two I forgot to breathe, almost suffocated. Life became so imbecilic that I rushed straight to the doctor, a plastic surgeon, who said, "Don't worry! With new discoveries, we change a person's face by surgery and the inside of his head with electronic rays. We can fill the brain with every type of knowledge like a tape recorder. That's probably the smartest thing to do, the best way to give you knowledge nowadays. After enlargement, commensurate with the desired results, we decorate the inside of the head with appropriate knowledge. Different knowledge is required for different life-styles. The knowledge we give poor children would be useless to rich children. We teach some how to make money and some how to spend it. Why should we, for no reason, equip a person for making a million when he isn't going to be a millionaire? Everyone should acquire the knowledge that is needed in his capacity. What sense is there in teaching street-sweepers the art of kissing a lady's hand? Why should we poison the life of society? Let them live comfortably. Let the producers produce, the consumers consume. You have now left the producers and become a consumer. Your old knowledge is no longer useful. You must have new knowledge. What need does a person on a monthly wage have for higher mathematics?

Anyone Want a Million Dollars?

Why should we mix difficult calculations in a man's mind? Give a man a simple rule, that's all. 'Spend until your money's gone!' you say. When your money's gone, if the month isn't over, go to the bank and borrow. Continue spending! Men mustn't tire their minds with difficult questions unnecessarily. An overtired mind is of no use to anyone. The economic situation? What do you care, man! I said you're a consumer, leave that business to the producers. Let them poison their lives. Do you worry about the political situation? There's no value in being troubled about that. Let people with incomes worry about it. You look after getting along. Be a heroic soldier, a sergeant, a major, if you wish, a general!"

Friend, if I desired riches, I did so in order to be comfortable. They said it was impossible, I couldn't be rich with this head. I escaped from communist Czechoslovakia and came here to be free, to be rich, not to listen to all this damn palaver! I ignored all those fools surrounding me, turned a deaf ear and a blind eye to their games, and took care not to get cheated. I deposited the whole million in the bank.

The big German beer hall was teeming with customers. The tall skinny Czech was a regular, but I had seen him at the tavern that night for the first time. I asked his name and they told me, "Bearded Jenikov." He continued his story:

The bank director told me, "If you leave your money like that, in a few years you'll want for a single loaf of bread. Better you put this money to work."

How should I put it to work? I never saw more than a hundred dollars at one time before.

"Don't worry," the banker told me, "I have a friend who works in investments. Let me send you to him and he'll find a solution to your problem."

I went and found the director's friend. "Invest your money in sugar," he advised. "The price of sugar's going up." You know, I bought a half million dollars' worth of sugar. Well, six months later, I intended to sell the half million dollars' worth of sugar for a million. When I sold the sugar for *half* of what I'd paid, I realized how backward I was.

Before things got further out of hand, I went back to my doctor friend with a request: "Please! A new head!" The doctor took me to the electronic clinic. "Choose any head you like!" he said. On the shelves, row after row of head types. "How about this handsome head with curly hair; does it suit me?" I asked. "That womanizer head!" he replied. "That's for sex maniacs." I murmured, "Just let me catch that disease!"

With electronic rays, they rearranged my head and face to fit the model. How handsome, how pretentious I became, you wouldn't believe. I set afire nearly everything I touched. With one glance, I could almost light a cigarette, like sunlight through a magnifying glass. My insides were ablaze. I threw myself into the pool in the center of town. I sizzled like red-hot iron thrust into water. Steam streamed from my face and hands. Soon I would attack every woman who passed by. Life had become hell for me. At this point I visited the bank and checked on my balance. Half my money had melted away. I was losing my shirt. People were skinning me alive! The crooks would ruin me.

I returned to the clinic. "Please change the program on my head!" I begged. "It doesn't suit me at all. Make me a new knowledge program without changing my face." At the clinic, they showed me a flock of knowledge programs. T-model was the best fit. The T-model program said: "Thick-skinned. He thinks everything is created for him. The whole world was organized on his behalf. His greatest hobby is pleasure, eating and drinking. He has great faith in God. He makes merry."

I had always wanted to be thick-skinned. I thought that in this form my life would be very comfortable. I'd live the life of Riley! For a few weeks I lived like that. Oh, how nice! I ate, drank, and made merry. I didn't lift a finger to do a lick of work. Indolence and sloth were clearly my goals. Soon I'd take along a hired man to undo my fly when I went to the toilet. The strength disappeared from my legs. I lost the desire to do anything. People in the neighborhood I moved to all looked alike. All had salaried men to do their work. I wasn't comfortable unless up to my neck in debt. I didn't care how world politics or economics were going. I sat in front of the television watching variety shows from morning till night. Oh man, what a heavenly life!

I went to the clinic to ask why I was living in a dream filled with so much pleasure and delight. They told me that the head I wore now was designed for consumers. I had such a pleasure-filled life because in this world everything is produced for them.

Around this time, the bank statement showed that my balance was very low. There was nothing I could do, no way I could turn. The money in the bank was flowing away like water in the gutter. Before I was completely ruined, I visited the clinic again. "This can't go on!" I cried. "Make me a proper program so my money in the bank won't all be lost."

"First you must give up all your old habits," they said. "No television. No drinking Coke. No more chasing women. It's forbidden to follow changes in fashion. You must believe in personal freedom. You must read politics, history, and economics." Also, I was to learn how to buy low and sell high.

Damn such millions! Now, if I get sick, a doctor doesn't come to take care of me. Technicians arrive with hammers and screwdrivers. They take me to a garage to change my spare parts.

The bearded Czechoslovakian fell silent. Then he cursed the prime minister till the air turned blue, paid for the beer, and headed for the door.

Outside, an icy Canadian wind was blowing.

FAT TOM

We came on summer vacation to this village established on the shore of Silver Lake at the foot of Orford Mountain. A polar country, it never gets hot in the summer months! After all, ours is an imitation summer.

The locals scream, "I'm burning!" as soon as they see the sun. We too have fallen into their way of thinking. At home, our disrespectful neighbors, winter or summer, grab their luggage and take off for distant climes. These low-lifes complain about burning to a crisp under the sun here, then go to hotter climates in order to cool off. Escapees from the so-called summer heat, they rush off to Florida, near the equator, to get cooler. They disappear for two or three weeks as if into a black hole. Then they reappear, swarthy as Arabs. They consider sunburn a sign of wealth and experience.

Even in winter, the women bare their suntanned legs to the sun any old place, peeling them like bananas. They uncover their shoulders and shake their arms like wings. Whoever has the darkest skin is considered the best. She's known to be wealthier.

Man, what idiocy! We used to fear getting burned and avoided the sun. Obviously, times have changed.

At first, we said, "What nonsense!" But finally, we too felt we must conform. In fact, it was impossible not to conform! When we hadn't gone on summer vacation for three or four years, our neighbors began making fun of us. They thoroughly needled us. "What's wrong?" they asked. "Are you staying home because you're afraid somebody'll steal your money?" When they saw my wife, they'd kid her, saying, "Hope you get well soon; you should see the doctor! Goodness, anybody that pale needs medical attention!" There was no way out, friend. We were forced to go along with them or they wouldn't let us draw a peaceful breath in the neighborhood. When they left my wife alone, they ridiculed me. In the morning on the bus, the neighborhood guys asked, "Are you going to buy a new house with all that money you save every month?" I didn't answer. What can be said to such stupid remarks? If it hadn't gone any further, OK. But they also gave our daughters a bad time at school. "Boy, your father's tight," they said. "Just look at your face. There's more color in a ripe lemon. Yellow probably runs in your family. It's probably inherited by all of you."

Finally I'd had enough; I was fed up with their jibes. I told my wife, "Now it's our turn. We'll find a good spot and go on summer vacation." When one of our friends said, "Go to Silver Lake. It's a very nice, tidy place. You'll enjoy it," we took his advice and came here to this village.

We liked the place on sight. The whole village was spick-and-span—not a scrap of paper in the streets. Flowers were planted everywhere. People smiled and were pleasant. Everything was as orderly as a clock. The whole population dressed neatly; even their shoes were brand new. I was glad we came. Man, we had it made! We'd stay here a month. I'd go to bed late, get up late, and read all day. I'd go on walks. A whole month of freedom! A vacation from the pitiless rat-race in the city! Free of the rush and struggle! The world was mine! A whole month of joy!

I went outside and filled my lungs with the lake air. I just about strangled from coughing. Lord, my lungs had become so estranged from clean air! It bothered me as much as smoke. But the biggest change was the silence. We would be rescued from the city's clamor. Even if only for a month, we would be free of the noise of planes, trains, buses, radios, and television.

The first day was spent getting settled. We walked around and memorized the names of streets and shops. The next morning when we awoke, we found two bottles of fresh milk, fresh cheese, hot bread, and a basket of apples at our door. The food was very clean, delicious, and had been placed carefully in the basket. A card had been attached, "Welcome to our village. Eat hearty!" signed "Fat Tom." Fat Tom must be the milkman bidding us welcome. No doubt he'd drop in later to collect for the milk and cheese. My wife said,

Fat Tom

"These must be a gift! They give the first day's milk and cheese free to get your business."

Near evening, a small child appeared at the door, an envelope in his hand. "Are you the renters in this house?" he asked. Upon my answer of "Yes!" he gave me the envelope. I opened it and found two movie tickets and a card saying "With best wishes, Fat Tom." This Fat Tom must not only be the milkman but also the man who runs the movie. Evidently he wants to establish a friendship with us. What else could it be? Is it proper for someone to give us gifts like this? After all, I'm not his brother! What's it to him if I come from a big city? Maybe he's confused me with some rich guy.

That evening, curious about Fat Tom, we went to the movie but couldn't spot him there. It was good we went, though, because it was a nice theater. You really couldn't call it a village movie, the film had won an Oscar last year and was very popular. I asked the person sitting beside me if he knew Fat Tom. "Please!" he said, "don't say Fat Tom. He calls himself Fat Tom but he wants us to call him Mr. Tom."

When we returned from the movie, we found a thick envelope by the door. It informed us of the meetings and events organized for the following day. In the morning at the small village motel, there was a special breakfast prepared from apples grown in the village. They had sent enough tickets for each of us. Events that would take place after breakfast also were announced. For example, there was a museum to see. Tickets providing entrance to the museum were added. Later on, a barbecue was being given at the village hotel. Coupons for lunch had also been included. All this was from Fat Tom.

After receiving this envelope, our anxiety about Fat Tom grew even greater. Who could he be? At most, Fat Tom must be a spendthrift, someone devoted to doing good. Otherwise, what sense was there in his undertaking all this expense? Finally, I was a foreigner from the city. Perhaps there was no one in this village as worldly or sophisticated as I. But no one would throw money away merely because a man was sophisticated. Maybe these villagers thought I was a nobleman because of my speech and dress. It just could be! Nothing's impossible. Didn't my departed mother use to say, "You must have been born to a good family"? Maybe the poor woman

Fat Tom

bore me without being conscious of my nobility. If you look at it basically, nobility becomes me. Maybe our next-door neighbor spread the word to the villagers. "Such and such a very important person lives here." Fat Tom heard this and showed us the necessary interest. If that's true, bravo to Fat Tom! He is currying my favor. He certainly knows a person's worth. I knew that things would turn out like this someday. I had sensed that society would understand my secret. I told my wife, "We must live up to the respect being paid us. No yelling just anywhere. We must always dress clean and neat. Tell the children not to fight or make noise. Don't let them forget to say, 'Yes, sir, no, sir, thank you, sir!' when they talk."

The next morning I rose early. The out-of-doors glowed. I went out to tour the village. Walking in the brisk morning air made me happy. Within four or five minutes I was outside the village. Where houses ended, small farms and orchards began. In the morning coolness, the peasants were working incessantly. I stopped and said, "Hello!" to the villager beside a fence. He didn't answer or even raise his head. "Good Lord, I wonder if the man's deaf!" Had I perhaps, unknowingly, somehow been rude? He must not know me. He fails to answer a great person whom the whole village had rushed to greet and honor. It's out of the question. When I looked at him a little more closely, I could see that this was the smiling citizen who sat beside me at the movie. I had met this man again at the museum and the dining room. We'd conversed in a friendly, sincere manner. He had been so friendly and nice that both my wife and I had been astonished. Now see the ingrate! He acts as if he doesn't recognize me. How quickly people forget their friends! But who had accepted the invitations of these poor people? Who had listened to their rustic nonsense and laughed at their jokes? I had! "Go to hell!" I muttered and left.

A little farther on, I saw two peasants feeding their cows. "Good morning!" I called. One of them, with a half smile, answered, "Good morning." The other peasant took his arm and pulled him away. There must be some hidden point in this business. The people must be afraid of me. They must have taken me for the president of some other country. I wondered who they thought I was.

Fat Tom

Farther on I chanced across a villager hoeing tomatoes. He hoed without pause. When I said, "Hello!" he answered, "Hello!" I had a couple of questions to ask him but he said, "Please don't talk to me! If Fat Tom sees, he'll clobber me! It's working hours now. When talking time comes, I'll talk to you." "Come on, friend," I said, "how could that be! Tom's a nice easy-going man. You should see what nice things he's done for us." "Please!" the man insisted, "Leave now, I'll come tonight and explain."

Eagerly I waited for it to get dark. At night the villager came. Again he was pleasant and smiling, "Forgive me, I couldn't talk this morning. I had a lot of work to do and if I'd talked, I couldn't have finished it in time."

"So if you don't finish on time what happens, brother, what's wrong with finishing three or four minutes late?"

"Please, *that's* the worst thing!" he said. "Not to finish your work on time is a crime, but to work during the time set aside for consumption of village production is a bigger crime. For us, the biggest sin is to produce during the hours set aside to consume. During consumption time a person must consume, during production time he must produce. If all goes smoothly like this, no rows or quarrels occur. Look, I'll tell you how we established this:

"In the olden days, we were very poor. When Tom came to our village, everything changed. One day he said, 'Come, let's play a game. In a short time, we'll all be rich. Even if we're not rich, none of us will remain poor.' Then, he explained the game to us. We would divide the day in two. Half would be set aside for consumption, the other half for production. 'Every day, whatever you consume, consume twice as much and make twice as much. Don't worry about not having any money. Enter a shop and take whatever you need. Go to the tailor and have him sew you a suit, to the restaurant and eat your fill. Everyone must seriously embrace this game. Previously, we have considered production more important than consumption. As a matter of fact, if consumption is insufficient what good is production? Watch how soon we all live in comfort.'

"First we said, 'Is this man crazy or what?' but we were so bad off we decided to give it a try. In the beginning everyone feared bartering. This was unheard of. Could circumstances change by a

Fat Tom

person giving goods and property free? Just let me tell you how rich it made us!

"For example, I had a small garden that I worked all year. I couldn't sell half the tomatoes I raised; they stayed in the field and rotted. I couldn't even take them to the city to sell because everyone raised tomatoes in his own yard. When the tomatoes all ripened at the same time you never saw such bounty. In the village, too, the grocer, tailor, barber, and milkman all raised vegetables in their own gardens. When Tom came up with this game, I had the tailor make me a suit. I wore free clothes for the first time. Before I left the tailor's shop, his wife had arrived at our garden and taken twenty kilos of tomatoes. She told my wife, 'The day after tomorrow, I want twenty kilos more.' When I went to the barber, he lost no time in frequenting my house for eggs, meat, and tomatoes. When I got sugar and flour from the grocer, he raised Cain with our lambs and chickens. The barter that started out slowly like that, speeded up later unbelievably. The people in trying to outsmart others started to eat and wear things they'd never eaten or worn before. We stopped drinking water and drank nothing but milk. I had my house painted three times this year. What with paint, doctor, and midwife being free, we've had four children in four years!

"The beginning and end of this business is Fat Tom. He arranges the entire operation. If someone spoils the fun by not producing the desired product, he is instantly thrown out of the village. If the milkman has too much milk, he is punished. 'Everything must be in balance!' says Tom. 'Too much production is worse than too little production.' Therefore, everyone looks after the disposition of his goods.

"Before you came to the village, everything was fine. We lacked only one thing. Now that you have come, that deficiency is corrected."

"What do you want me to do?" I asked.

"You used to be a toilet cleaner, didn't you?"

"Yes," I replied.

"Great!" he said. "There's been no toilet cleaner in this village. We were very worried about who would clean things up if someday the sewer gave us trouble. Therefore, we took you into our village with great affection and sent you gifts. Now, if someone's toilet gets clogged, you'll no doubt get the job."

"But I just came here on a month's vacation!" I said.

"No matter!" he replied. "All our toilets plug up this month."

NAKED YULA

(After I thought of the Naked Yula incident, Jerry told me that such a tale had been written two thousand years ago. "Good Lord!" I said to myself. "Two thousand years, and people still haven't been able to learn the differences between the naked and the clothed!")

Yula was sitting in the middle of the three-hundred-store Bonaventure Shopping Centre—stark naked. This was an image hard to believe but sweet to see. At the center of the high-columned mall, on a bench, she was reading a magazine. She had chosen the busiest spot in the mall. The place where she sat was visible from every corner of the bazaar. On one side of her were shops selling books, phonograph records, shoes, and women's apparel; on the other, men's clothing and skiing equipment were sold and there was also an eating place.

    In the center of all these shops, Naked Yula was so naked, so innocent, that people walking by thought the girl sitting on the bench to be a marble statue. Everyone rushed about his work and business, indifferent to what he saw. Civilized people. They were accustomed to seeing a naked mannequin in the middle of the Bonaventure Shopping Centre. But no one was accustomed to seeing this kind of nakedness. Those who had come to the Bonaventure Shopping Centre were passing by, indifferent to what they saw, because they encountered this kind of nakedness only in the baths.

    Tendril Yula was eighteen years old, carnation-white, wind-fluid, tomato-pink. As she read the magazine in her hand, May was coming, rain was leaving her upturned breasts. On her face was a natural, ingenuous look. Yula was totally a child. Like afternoon air, Yula's sunny body was peaceful and silent. Free, happy, soft. I looked into

Naked Yula

her eyes. She didn't see me. She was lost in her magazine. She was not moved by splashing pool water, flight of garden birds, or fluttering of leaves. In Yula was the happiness of calm water.

Two young pharmacists were the first to behold this vision. When they saw Yula like that, they instantly knew she was stark naked because they were familiar with a woman's body. They rushed outside. Employees in the ladies' apparel store who saw them running also rushed out and surrounded Yula on all sides. People wandering about the shopping center also gathered in the mall. The owner of the ladies' apparel store, asking, "Who carried our mannequin out here?" walked right up to Yula. He wanted to put her back in the show window. When the department store sales clerks explained that the one sitting on the bench was a naked girl, the old man ran back to the store to get his glasses. Curious as to what this nakedness was, the crowd grew around Yula. A holiday air enveloped the Bonaventure Shopping Centre. People were happy over this event.

On a Saturday morning in the middle of winter, everyone forgot his interest in the world outside, forgot the mud, snow, and cold, and found happiness in the body warmth of a young girl of eighteen.

The store owner looked with pleasure at the gradually growing crowd. He had never expected that the shopping mall could bring this many people together at one time. It was a source of satisfaction. Previously the center had remained distant from the mainstream. The thought of their store's being off the beaten path worried the owners. Today's event made them all smile.

The crowd filling the mall had flowed from neighboring streets and other stores. Department store customers, as soon as they'd finished their shopping, rushed to the mall where naked Yula was. The crowd surrounding her became enormous. Stores were emptied. Shopping came to a halt. When sales stopped, the owner of the men's shoe store, seeing that an idle crowd wasn't profitable, became angry.

"Look at that, would you! All the stores are empty. No one is shopping. Throw this woman out of here. Call the police to take her away. We can't put up with such immoral conduct!" he yelled.

A young man beside him said, "Now, just forget this police business, old man! Have you ever seen such a beautiful body before? Look, it's as if carved from marble."

Naked Yula

The owner of the record store also chastised the angry man: "Are you crazy? Where will you find a greater ad than this? If you spent a million dollars you couldn't have better advertised yourself. Just wait a little. Watch how the radio and television media publicize our stores. In a week this place will be choked with customers!"

The angry man smiled a little.

Far from embarrassing, Yula's body was like a spring—water for the thirsty, shade for the tired, food for the hungry. The hills of her breasts, rising and falling like a bellows, fanned the scent of flowers like a zephyr. Her tremulous breasts were a purple flood then white ebb of the tides.

People gathered around the girl whispered to each other but didn't talk to her. It was as if they were afraid of startling and scaring this beautiful virgin away. No one said anything to her. There was a mysterious vacuum between the girl and the crowd.

I said to myself, "Why are all these people silent? Isn't there one among them without virtue? Let one make a crack at this tender, April-leaf girl . . . just let him say the girl's naked! But what a bunch of lethargic youths! In my younger days, what fun we would have made of such a naked girl, even joking a little about the looks of her legs. We would have made a pass, but, brother, these young guys are dead!"

OK, let's say there is no one unmannerly among these people; isn't there anyone who feels sorry for her, either? The girl will soon die from catching cold. No one pays any attention. Look, the tips of the poor thing's breasts have turned purple. Mother! look at her legs; the hair's on end like a quince. No one says, "Oh, dear child, aren't you cold?" No one, as a father, a brother, a man, is about to act like a blanket and wrap and warm this girl. No one says, "What a pity, you're naked!"

Oh woe! As if people are made of stone! The crowd is cold potatoes, brother. And where are our brave youths? Look at that sweet navel, as white as a sugar cookie, shivering from the cold. I doubt that this generation will amount to anything. OK, let's say there are no brave men among them. Very well, are there no reactionaries or conservatives either? If it had been up to us, by God, we would have filled this unvirtuous woman full of holes. They say there's re-

Naked Yula

ligion and the Book on this earth, but in God's name, they turn them into a mockery. They could at least spit in her face and say, "You're naked!" I look at the crowd surrounding the girl. Among them there isn't one honest person who will say, "You're naked!" They're all a bunch of baaing lambs. Eat the grass from her hand and continue the baaing!

I felt sorry for the girl, stark naked in the bazaar. Thinking vaguely that I knew her, I approached.

"Hello!" I said.

"Oh, hello!" she replied, surprised at hearing my voice.

I was going to say, "Are you crazy? Should one sit here naked?" but changed my mind.

"You'll catch a chill, Yula," I said. "Where are your clothes?"

"I can't believe it! Could anyone catch a chill in this beautiful weather?"

"But, Yula, you're naked!" I said. "If you don't get dressed you'll get chilled!"

"Such poor manners! and he says 'naked' to me without embarrassment."

"Don't you see that you're exposed, naked all over?"

"Can you just show me where I'm naked?"

"My girl, wherever I point. Haven't you any eyes?"

"I can see. *Your* eyes are bad. I'm not naked or anything."

I looked at Yula. From her knees up, the girl's body, slowly broadening, opened out, became round at her hips, united at her waist, then, changing direction again, broadened at her breasts. Before my eyes was a pile of legs and hips.

"God forgive me!" I thought, "You can't argue with the present generation. Nobody listens. They recite what they already know and here's a typical example in front of me. Just look at this youngster!"

Two slim streams flow like rivers, then, in the north at the place where they meet, at the confluence, the water makes an eddy, a whirlpool, and, turning through the brush, widens at the navel. Yula was still saying, "I'm not naked!" but one couldn't undress more than this even for one's wedding night. She was being stubborn. "I'm not naked!" she insisted. "Touch!" she said. "Show me where I'm naked!" If I touched her someplace and said, "You're naked here!"

Naked Yula

I could get in a lot of trouble. but the girl had to understand she was naked or she would get sick. The girl had remained as fresh, sweet, and clean as God created her, as if untouched by human hand.

Unexpectedly, she turned to the crowd surrounding us and said:

"You're all witnesses! This man assaulted me with indecent remarks saying I'm naked. You say! Am I naked or is this man lying?"

While no one else opened his mouth to answer, the shop owners replied all together:

"This man is lying!"

Yula turned to me and said,"Now let's see if you can say I'm naked, that you're not lying!"

"You're naked!" I repeated.

"Call the police! I have a complaint against this man!" she yelled.

The increasing disturbance pleased the shop owners. As we were yelling back and forth, the crowd grew. Word of the incident spread throughout the Bonaventure Shopping Centre and spilled over into other stores. Hearing of the goings-on, people dropped what they were doing and rushed to see the naked girl. At this juncture, the police arrived. "Thank God, I'm rescued!" I said to myself. No doubt the police would see the facts. After all, they wouldn't lie. Certainly they would see that the girl was naked and summon her to the station. Yet, I was trying to understand Yula. She was looking at me with her breasts from the depth of her eyes. Large, erect, like two myrtle berries they stood white and moist. They burned with desire to suckle the sun. If I touched them, sunlight would squirt forth instead of milk.

Yula pointed me out to the police. "This man told me I'm naked. He molested me. All these people are witnesses."

The police looked at me.

"Did you tell this woman she was naked?"

Would you believe the police could botch things up so? Couldn't they see the girl's naked?

"Mr. Policeman," I said, "take a look. Isn't this woman naked?"

The policeman replied: "I'm neutral! It's not up to me to determine. I'm no expert on nakedness."

The police then turned to the crowd and asked:

"Did this man tell this girl she's naked and molest her?"

The crowd with one voice, in a chorus cried:
"He said it! He did it!"
I turned to the crowd and with all my strength screamed at them:
"Damn fools! You're nuts! You're nuts!"

AUTUMN IN MONTREAL

Muddy torrents grow violent and descend into the valley driving earth, limbs, and trees before them. Montreal heads toward fall dragging along women, yearning, love, colors, and fire. While jumping from season to season, the city leaves an acrid taste in the mouth. Women, like the smell of fresh coffee, float through the air; time burns the tongue. While streets change from day to night, light to darkness, wrinkles appear on faces; depression is felt in the heart. An indefinable something gone from inside people is replaced by a familiar emptiness. Time is finally overthrown.

At a gallery on Sherbrook Street, Turkey's Anatolia is being exhibited; Anatolian nights, donkeys, weddings, fishermen, and Karagöz puppets enliven the wall. Montreal looks at them in amazement.

Life in the fall, which flows along with the coming torrent, is caught and held. Then it flies off. The difference between the last of August and the first of September isn't just a day; it's a season. The water of August turns to fire in September. The green trees turn yellow, crimson, then bare. Water, no longer blue, turns gray, then muddy. The ground is stripped bare and changes to dirt again.

The difference between the art of two countries isn't just a matter of colors; the civilizations also are involved. Thanks to our friends, they squeezed great Anatolia onto a few canvases and shipped them here. Sherbrook takes me back home. Blue from the Aegean, quince-yellow from Antalya . . . Hello, my lemon-blossom Mersin!

The colors flow like cool, bubbling spring water. The purple of the sky darkens, water turns lifeless, murky, then becomes actual night. Red turns into fire and climbs the trees. In the gallery on Sherbrook, Turkish art engulfs the city in poetry. The gallery owner is a friend of mine who agreed to exhibit the Turkish paintings even

Autumn in Montreal

though they were not for sale. "Even though we aren't permitted to sell them, they'll attract a lot of visitors," he said.

All the artists' works are gathered here. Last week Nuri Abaç had a personal show. This week we have Abaç, Atmaca, Pesen, T. Erol, Islimyeli, Gökçebağ, and Kesinok. Those who enter the gallery look at the works in bewilderment. Not all the works could be hung at one time. Only a small corner was available.

A middle-aged woman in the gallery was shopping for a suitable picture frame. When she saw the oil in my hand, she looked into my eyes with a gaze as warm as a summer breeze and smiled, a beautiful woman. She had expertly erased the wrinkles of time from her face.

"Very nice!" she said.

"Thank you!" I replied.

When the gallery owner warmly welcomed me with open arms, the woman's smile grew even friendlier. She approached me again, interested in further conversation.

"Would you tell me something?" she asked. "I like this artist's work but I'm not familiar with his name. If you're leaving, let's walk together. Please tell me a little about him."

We left and walked in the warm evening sunshine. My hands shook. She must have been ten years younger than I. Her black eyes sparkled as she spoke in her Middle-European accent.

"Where are you from?" I asked.

"Hungary," she replied.

"So you're a Hungarian!"

She giggled. "And you?"

"Turkish! Would you care for a glass of wine?"

Ha! Drinking wine in the Sherbrook sunshine at a sidewalk cafe! To hell with the bank! There must be more to life than that! Bank employee number 670-250 died! Passed away! Then and there my former self returned! Where was this woman twenty or twenty-five years ago? She talked and explained. My memory turned into a grasshopper; I leaped way back in time. Suddenly the weather was crisp and clear. The sun became wine in crystal. Young once again, I was sitting with the Hungarian woman and talking.

Autumn appeared in the city. They said it came yesterday; a

Autumn in Montreal

red fall reaching into the depths. The woman was telling me about Budapest. She loved pictures very much. "I almost became a painter!" she declared.

A few drops of rain sticking to the pane trickled down. The drops brought a coolness to the air. I held her hands. They were warm—Hungarian hands.

Daydreaming, I was a shy twenty-year-old, free as a bird. She should see me now. What a surprised Hungarian from Budapest she'd be! She talked without looking at me. "Who?" she might say; "This man!" and maybe she could mistake me for someone else. No, my friend, how could she! After all, nothing in a Hasmet Akal painting reminded me of me. This young man was idiotic. "It will never come again," they told the youth. "What won't come again?" "Autumn!" they said. From now on, the leaves won't fall, there won't be a shedding of leaves in the parks and hills. The sun won't disappear from the foam on Mediterranean shores. Mersin will remain a little fishing village. It will be April and May all year.

Fall didn't come for a long time. With my hands in my pockets, I created spring. "Place the green like this!" I said. "Spread the blue here. That's not enough. Spread plenty, even more!" The woman was listening to me. "Let everyone see the sky!" I said. "Spread yellow here; not that, break an egg, pour it on! It needs light, sunshine!"

The woman giggled and squeezed my hand. "Put a heart here!" I said. We laughed together. "Make it a greedy heart!" she said.

I left the woman and returned to my present self.

While we were together, she was a bunch of violets with delicate shoulders. What was her name, anyway? "What's a married woman to you?" someone asked.

On another street, she was a basket of cherries with narrow skirts and warm hands. I was embarrassed but the embarrassment didn't last long.

In another season, when she wore a white skirt, she was a jasmine sprout. She bloomed into jasmine. When I think of her, smoke still gets in my eyes.

EAGLE-EYE

Before he rode the mule, Blackfoot was a strange kind of Indian who laughed readily, was easily pleased, good-hearted, never bothersome, and had a sound bottom. In the village, only he was a friend of the children, playing with them, telling stories, and singing songs. He used to gather a group together and take them to the woods where he entertained them by showing how to track rabbits, hunt birds, and catch foxes. He taught them that rabbits, foxes, and wolves were children's friends.

He impressed on their minds which fruits in the forest could be eaten and which must not. Indians, he told them, loved the wind and rain. Without wind and rain, the grass wouldn't grow. "Wild cattle, bison, and buffalo don't grow without grass!" he used to say. Without bison the Indians would die from hunger. When the little Indians heard this, they laughed heartily. They used to beg Blackfoot, "Tell it again!" He could never turn the youngsters down.

The year Blackfoot was born, there was a great forest fire. Herds of animals, great and small, as well as the forest were burned; only the lives of eagles were spared. The Indian community, seeing this, understood the importance of being an eagle. That year the eagle symbol entered the native folk songs. When girls dreamed of love, when they thought of the marriage tent, they reserved a place for the eagle. They fantasized long, crooked noses for their men. That year was called "Year of the Eagle."

Well, that's how it happened! One wet-leaved spring day, when he was born in the rain, Blackfoot's mother gave him the name Eagle-eye. She wanted her son to have sharp eyes and broad wings.

Blackfoot didn't grow up according to his mother's wishes. Instead of wings, his feet grew. Instead of being handsome and majestic as an eagle, he became a timid brave with a short nose. Like the other Indians, he was quick to laugh and good-natured. He loved to wander the mountains and slopes and used to return from these useless wanderings with black feet, because of walking through old coal fields. In time, they named him Blackfoot.

The changing of his name from Eagle-eye to Blackfoot truly saddened his mother. All her bright hopes were destroyed. After his name change, Blackfoot stopped associating with other braves. No longer hunting wild cattle, bison, and buffalo on the mountains and plains, he frequented the forest, gathering flowers and fruit, watching birds, and tracking rabbits. As he gazed unhappily at the village children from a distance, sometimes a depression fell into his heart, the reason for which he couldn't understand. On such days he preferred gathering flowers in the forest.

Evenings, he returned to the village with a song on his lips, blackened with coal to the knees, his hands full of flowers. He brought his mother fruit gathered in the forest. Blackfoot's mother worried about him. "If things go on this way, I won't be able to find him a wife," she complained. Blackfoot's situation provided a lot of amusement for the village young people.

When his mother told Blackfoot of her worries, he laughed. "Mother!" he said, "You're worried about nothing. I'm happy with my life. Thank God I have no problems or troubles. Do I have to go hunting like the other young men? They go, but what do they do? Do they find game every day? They don't, do they? Don't I find food every day?"

His mother said, "My son, if you go on like this, the girls won't marry you. Listen to me! No father wants to give his daughter to a ne'er-do-well like you. In their eyes, you're not an important person."

Blackfoot always shrugged his shoulders at these words.

Twenty times since his birth, the rivers in the valley had carried water from the melting snow in surrounding mountains to the great blue river. Blackfoot had now reached maturity and become a sturdy man.

The little Indians who had once gone to the forest with him had also grown and become hunters. The little girls were bigger, too.

Eagle-eye

Some were brides, some mothers. As the days and years passed, Blackfoot's circle of friends had thinned out. Things had gone bad.

Not only his mother's voice but also a voice inside him repeated to Blackfoot that he was a tentless bachelor. He was filled with uneasiness. He felt like an ant crushed under a giant foot. Beset by sadness, he just let everything take its course. He passed the days easily. In the mountains, in the wilds, and on the riverbanks, time flowed by while he still pursued flowers and birds. The nights, though, were distressing. Like an old woman, time wouldn't get up and move from where she was sitting.

This last year's spring had come in a flood. All the trees on the riverbank were wrapped in pink flowers. The Indian's friend, wind, turned the trees to fire. The river water flowed along calling and shouting. A wild spring, this...

Like the spring, Blackfoot's heart was colorful and breezy. At the same time he was angry with the village people. He silenced his bad heart and awakened the good one. He gathered flowers and brought them to his mother as a present on days the old Indian was sad.

One day on the mountain slopes, he saw a mule stretched out on the ground. He had never before seen such an animal. It wasn't difficult to capture the sick mule collapsed there on the ground.

He brought the mule grass and water. For three weeks, without a break, he looked after the mule like a mother. Finally the mule recovered and got to its feet. Blackfoot thought deeply. What was he going to do with this animal? Could it be eaten? Suddenly, the old stories of aged heroes came to mind. According to the old ones, beyond the seashore, where the sun set, the Indians had a great domesticated animal, like a dog, that ran fast and never tired. It was easy to hunt with them. The possibility of doing this with the mule he had found crossed his mind.

Blackfoot hid the mule in a cave on the mountain. He didn't want to take him to the village until he had found a use for the animal. He made a rope and tied it around the mule's neck.

First, Blackfoot sat on the animal like sitting on a chair. When the mule walked, he ended up on the ground. On the second try, he let his legs hang on both sides of the animal. With the rope in his hand, he went through the forest on the mule.

Riding high above the ground, Blackfoot felt strong and powerful. From where he sat, he could see the forest more easily. He said to himself, "I have made the forest beautiful!" He could also see farther. "My eyes have become sharper!" he said. The mule began to trot and moved like lightning among the trees. Blackfoot loved this speed. "I'm the fastest person in the village!" he cried. That day, he rode until evening on the mule. Then, he felt a pain in his bottom. His behind was all sores and bruises because he was unused to riding bareback. He was crushed and angry at the villagers. He was going to take out his pain on them because these bruises had happened on their account.

The happy smile slowly disappeared from his face. Instead of the good-natured one who laughed at everything, there appeared a cross Indian with sore buttocks. All of this had happened because of those timid braves in the village.

He was also angry with himself. Why, like an idiot, had he taken flowers to his mother all those years? He was a moron, that's why! Would a man this smart, this capable, do such idiotic things? But he had.

He looked up at the Great Father in the sky. The winds blowing on earth were His. He looked down. "My name is Eagle-eye!" he declared. "Know this! If you want me, call me by this name! Otherwise, I won't come!"

No one seeing him so silent must think him incapable. He had been born Chief, he must be the leader.

He mounted the mule and headed for the village. Blackfoot, on top of the mule, was transformed into an eagle. His arms became feathered and grew into wings. His nose grew longer, crooked, and became a beak. His eyes grew small and hard. His feet shortened and became claws.

In the evening, Eagle-eye entered the village riding the mule.

When his mother saw the young eagle on the mule, she smiled with joy.

INGRATITUDE

Outside, the machines continued rattling and clicking. For four days the city had been out of adjustment and unregulated. The "tick-tocks" of the giant clock were irregular. There was a change of harmony in the emanations of clicks. There were jumps and slips. When these emanations changed, city life changed too.

That beautiful Saturday, while city people were enjoying themselves in the park or shopping, somehow the giant clock's sound rhythms changed. Everyone collapsed where they were, like puppets with broken strings.

When it happened to me, I had all kinds of trouble. It being my day off, I was taking a bath. Just as I'd soaped my head well, the tick-tock of the clock stopped. At that instant, I stopped, "clunk," like a toy whose spring had wound down. My head wouldn't work. I was empty inside . . . My God, what was I doing here? Who was I? "Let me look in the mirror to see who I am," I said. But if I opened my eyes, I'd get soap in them. If I kept them closed, I couldn't see anything. If I could bathe, I'd bathe!

People get used to those tick-tocks. Addiction is worse than insanity, they say. When the ticking stopped, so did the thinking in my brain. "The cupboard was bare . . ." Thus I came out of the bathroom with my head soaped. Feeling with my hands, my eyes closed, I made my way to the sitting room. When my wife saw me, she screamed at the top of her lungs, "Oh my God, look at that imbecile; he's put his shorts on his head!"

"Where?" I replied in confusion. Without the tick-tocks, her head probably wasn't working, either. She'd become a complete idiot. As for me, I sat down with my soapy head and sang a sad ditty.

Ingratitude

As soon as the clock started ticking regularly again, I remembered where I was. What a blessing there was no one at home other than my wife. I ran back to the bathroom without being disgraced.

Others got into difficulties. Our friend Korbir Çalişkan was on the public sidewalk. "A very upsetting situation occurred," he said. However, he wouldn't explain what happened. Clearly it was too embarrassing.

Also that day, departure times for trains and airplanes became mixed up. Buses, subways, and trolleybuses took passengers in the wrong direction. Furthermore, they couldn't find their way home. Law-abiding citizens entered the homes of strangers. Thinking it his own, every one of them entered someone else's house. Not one was aware of his mistake until the ticks were back in order.

Some of my friends told of comical incidents that happened in the city before the ticking of the giant clock returned to its normal rhythm. They opened their eyes and when they became aware that the fat, ugly broad facing them was not their wife, they ran screaming into the streets. Many wore clothes that didn't belong to them or woke up in someone else's bed in a strange house. Thank heaven, most everyone faced these mistakes with great maturity. Can you imagine what would have happened to them in the old days? God forbid, there would have been much bloodshed. There used to be ideals like jealousy, honor, and virtue. Anyway, in our day, concepts like these rest on very advanced theories.

The Tuesday breakdown created even worse results. That day, the country's industry broke down. The factories were useless and produced defective goods. What can you do? You have to close one eye to such things on occasion. That inauspicious Tuesday, brewery technicians boarded the wrong bus and went to the city cemetery. Clock-factory workers were transported to the waterworks. Corpses were deposited at the flower market in the town square instead of the cemetery. Police surrendered convicts, who were supposed to be taken to prison, to a bank's central branch. Everything was topsy-turvy. Unhappily, "No machine is perfect." Wise men say, "Everything made by man develops a flaw."

Soon it will be ten years since we were rescued from the old, disorganized system. In spite of this, we still have such breakdowns

Ingratitude

from time to time. Basically, a regulated system controlled from the top is a good organization. So don't worry about such breakdowns in the operation of the giant clock.

The entire economy of the country is under the clock's control. Radio and television stations broadcast its ticks. Newspapers, magazines, and books publicize these sounds. Its ticks are the lifeline of the nation. The control of the country's industry depends on this system. Assisted by it, industrial production has increased ten times in the past ten years. Our country has developed from a primitive agricultural country to an advanced industrial nation. We are indebted to these sounds for this rapid development.

Today, in our homeland, we can produce two automobiles, three tanks, and four airplanes each minute. From the breweries, three thousand bottles of beer. We made three thousand pairs of shoes, four large ships, six thousand watches, three hundred shrouds, the same number of coffins, eighty thousand pins, and ten thousand shorts. Such production is due to a speedy and organized effort. Our scientists created today's ticks to speed up production. The ticks are broadcast twenty-four hours a day. Just as fishermen pull on their ropes in unison with a rhythmic "Heave ho, heave ho!" city radios, with their tick-tocks, are careful to start the people working slowly at first, then gradually increase the tempo.

The ticks hypnotize society. A person becomes a satellite and can work the whole day without tiring. The pulse beat, which conforms to these ticks, keeps our bodies healthy and reduces heart attacks. Thus, the death rate has decreased.

Naturally, it wasn't easy to learn to conform. At first, there were deaths. Some people lost their minds and jumped out of windows. Some ran all day, foundered, then died from exhaustion like horses.

Basically, it is a useful system. After the ticking became established, it was impossible for the lazy to swim against the current. In the brains of those who opposed it, it created great agitation. Many went deaf from the sound. There was no escape! It rang in one's ears day and night. Radio, television, loudspeakers, newspapers all cooperated in these broadcasts. We've put an end to laziness! All work like bees. The sounds are everywhere! At home, at the market, at the movies, in the toilet, in bed! Sound fills the air like dust,

Ingratitude

like the buzzing of flies . . . All this comes from one center. There must be no breakdown in work! If pin, tank, or shorts production broke down, if it fell below the announced plan, the country would be in dire straits.

Without pins, none of the clothing factories could work. Without clothes production, people would go into the streets naked, get sick, or lose their morals. If tank production ceased, things would be even worse. After all, our neighbors, the enemy, have been looking for an opportunity to occupy us. Can you imagine a breakdown in the production of shorts? Please, God, save us from that day!

A stop or delay is impossible! Let's assume beer production fell to a level below that anticipated. Then just come and look at the nighthawks. They'll take the next day off and beat their wives. Rubbish everywhere you look . . . There's no way out . . .

From the baker to the gravedigger, everything is arranged. Statistics show that three hundred people die each hour. Three hundred per hour are born. We feed this information into the system. It's very simple. If one lives to age ninety-seven, he turns in his "Central People's Committee" citizenship card. Without a card, a citizen can buy nothing at the market. Then this aged citizen, according to plan, must close his eyes and die within one or two weeks. While on one hand, three hundred people die, on the other, the "Central Committee" is prepared to replace them. Three hundred young couples mate to produce sprouts. Only with the greatest difficulty was the committee able to teach this to the citizenry. Quite a number of young citizens objected. They wanted to choose a mate in the traditional manner. We solved the problem with tick-tocks, but not easily.

I'm happy! I adapted to this organized life-style quickly! Here is a synopsis of my life's story: I'm an energetic, healthy, and happy human being. Don't worry about my age. Every morning at eighteen past seven, I awaken. At nineteen past seven, I look in the mirror and smile. Doctors say that it's efficacious to smile mornings. Therefore I smile twenty-two separate times per day. At twenty-seven past seven I take my sunbath. A two-minute sunbath keeps me vigorous. It kills microbes on my body. (I must remember to change the lamps in my sunlamp soon. Old bulbs don't give good light.) At

Ingratitude

twenty-nine past seven, I breakfast. At seven thirty-one, my bus comes. My entire day passes deliberately like that. I live without irritation or exasperation. There's no getting angry or swearing! No standing in line, no shortages, no excesses, no political quarrels!

Brother! what unregulated lives we lived in our youth: Try to catch the bus! Get to work on time! A person couldn't regulate where he was or what he was doing. The boss gets mad, I get fired. The landlord gets mad, I get thrown out of my house. The grocer gets mad and sells me bad food. In those days, it was as if God created people so they could cheat one another.

Yesterday, I went to the General Directorate for the Extension of Citizen's Lives. I saw a friend of mine there who worked in some capacity or other. With his help, I examined my file. Permission had been granted for me to live until the year 2030. Because I was a model citizen, my life had been extended three years. I returned home filled with pleasure.

"To live is a nice thing," I said to myself. In a few days spring would arrive in our city. Trees, flowers, and children would be everywhere. Yesterday, the mayor announced March 12 as tree-leafing day. That day, as every year, all trees would sprout leaves. The birds would begin to sing again. As for me, a sixty-five-year-young man, without asking anything from anybody, I'd turn into a horse and whinny. Wow, it's sweet to be alive!

In two days, the municipal tick-tocks begin their spring broadcasting. Then we'll provision ourselves at the stores and markets with everything we need. I'm going to live high this year!

At home I informed the wife of my joy. Unexpectedly, instead of being happy at my good fortune, she asked, "How long am *I* going to live?"

When I said, "I don't know," she muttered, "That damn government sticks its nose into everything. They even force a person who might wish to die in peace to live a long life!"

Would you just look at that dear wife of mine! Dammit, I thought we'd abolished jealousy. How stupid could I be? New order or old, it's all the same if a person's ungrateful. . . .

DOCTOR ISMAIL DÜZER

May God grant you never fall into the hands of a nurse or tax agent. There's no escape. They'll take your money or your life. I don't know where they find these stony-hearted tax agents. These low-down collectors look for a man to skin. I used to be afraid to go past the tax office. I would always go another way. They can go to the devil for all I care.

I'm sorry for the good Doctor Ismail Düzer. He must be in a really tight spot. When I see him rushing back and forth, looking neither right nor left, my heart aches. If I had the chance, I'd help him out. He's not run-of-the-mill. He's a well-known, well-bred man, a member of the university faculty. He has earned the love and respect of society.

After I had seen him for two days in a row dragging his feet up the wide steps to the tax office and then coming back down in a flurry, the feeling awakened in my heart to help dear Düzer.

After six months of unemployment, the last slap lowered on me by destiny was the offer of employment at the Montreal Tax Office. I said I would just as soon pass on that one, but it wasn't to be. The Employment Office informed me that if I didn't accept, they would cut off my insurance payments. I preferred working at the tax office to going hungry so that's why I thought I might be able to help dear old Düzer.

Evidently the employees couldn't reach an agreement when he came those two days in a row, because after he left the second time, they called me to their office.

This is how the agents, Mr. Richard and Mr. Gerin, explained Düzer's situation. Regardless of how well Dr. Düzer knew English, he still didn't understand tax terminology and left Mr. Gerin's questions without proper answers. The tax office employees were amazed at Dr. Düzer's erudition, refinement, and breeding. Bearing in mind that a person with a doctor's degree wouldn't make these kinds of errors, they found it fitting to include me in the investigation.

Since Düzer was an honest man, they wanted me to ask him a few questions in Turkish and learn the real situation before assessing him with any penalty.

The next morning, the honorable Ismail Düzer arrived at the tax office at ten o'clock. He was smartly dressed. Geniality and refinement shone from his face. His every aspect showed him to be a civilized man. I accompanied him and the two employees into the office where the interview was to be held.

Mr. Gerin began the discussion.

"Dr. Düzer, today we will examine the expense section of your tax return. We have two questions on this subject. If you recall, the return you prepared lists funeral expenses for your fathers for the years 1972, '73, and '74. How could this be?"

"You're absolutely right, sir. We don't know how it could be, either. My poor mother was very sad about it. Just think a moment, is it easy to lose three husbands in three years? May God keep you far from such trouble."

Gerin: "Dr. Düzer, I'm not asking you how these people died."

"Believe me, I don't know either, sir. I wasn't there. I heard the news by letter. One of them I like very much. He was a very good man. The other was very old. He died of that."

"Dr. Düzer, I'm not interested in your father's age. What I want to know is how it happened that you had three fathers. Are you sure you don't have another father left?"

"Ah, don't ask. It's a sad situation, isn't it? Now I'm considered an orphan. I don't think I'll have another father. If my mother doesn't marry again I can definitely say, 'I have no other father.' But if the Canadian government objects to my mother marrying again, I could prevent it. I'll do anything you order me to do!"

Gerin: "No, my friend, we don't want to interfere with your mother's remarrying."

"Thank you!"

Richard: "Dr. Düzer, did you really have three fathers?"

Doctor Ismail Düzer

"Do you think I would lie to an estimable man like you? I truly did have three golden-hearted fathers. Unfortunately, they all died."

"Very well, is it possible in Turkey for a woman to marry three men at the same time?"

"You mean, you're hinting that my mother lived with these men without being married. If someone else had said that, I truly would have been very angry. But I can't be angry with you. We like Canadians very much. In our homeland, too, Canadians are well thought of. It's the Americans we hate."

The two tax men scratched their heads in frustration.

Ismail Düzer continued: "Dear sirs, if you'll look in my file, you'll find three mukhtar certificates. In these documents it is announced that my three fathers died."

"Yes, we saw those. But we couldn't find any evidence that these men were married to your mother nor in what way these fathers were bound to your mother."

"You can be sure, dear friend, that they were bound by love. They lived loving each other so much that we young people watched with a desire to emulate them. In spite of their lives being nearly over, they always showed each other great respect."

Richard: "OK, how was it that three men could be married at the same time to one woman?"

"It's very hard! Because of this, my poor mother suffered a lot of troubles. Each of her husbands was a separate problem. One was a drinker. She suffered a lot because of that. He didn't come home at night. When he did come he was drunk. The other was a conductor on the train. He was on the road six days a week. She was always waiting for him. Ah, you can't realize what that poor woman suffered before we were finally raised! What she went through to get us a good education! You think this little help I'm giving her too much? Her third husband was a farmer. He had a tiny farm. The whole year, winter and summer, he never left his land. Would you call that living together?"

Mr. Gerin and Mr. Richard looked at each other in astonishment. Mr. Gerin: "Dr. Düzer, let's scrutinize this problem from the beginning. From your view, you have three fathers. One of these fathers dies each year. You claim you spent five hundred fifty dollars for

Doctor Ismail Düzer

funeral expenses on each father. The statements, documents, and receipts you show are in order. We're just curious as to why these three people have different addresses."

"You're right! But what could I do? I couldn't force them all to live in the same city, after all!"

Gerin: "OK, are these three cities close to each others? Van, Kayseri, Izmir?"

"Naturally, they're very close. Kayseri is a two-hour journey from Van and Izmir is two hours from Kayseri. So you can see, if these three people wanted, they could be together in two hours. Would you call that far?"

So it was that at this point Mr. Gerin turned to me and said, "Ask Dr. Düzer in Turkish whether or not a person could have three fathers."

When dear Düzer realized that I knew Turkish, the expression on his face changed. The lines on his face and his look grew hard. He turned to me:

"I find your knowing Turkish and not mentioning it unmannerly. I don't think it necessary for me to remind you that the personal information you heard here is secret. Ignore what I told these two idiot tax employees. I hadn't thought that these guys would be that insensitive. They don't know what's going on."

Putting pressure on Ismail Düzer, I asked: "OK, did you really have three fathers?"

"Watch your tongue, young man! Do you know to whom you are speaking? It would be a good idea if you found out with whom you are speaking before asking such a stupid question. I am one of our country's outstanding scholars. Watch your step!"

"I didn't say anything to belittle you. I simply asked if the information on your return was true or not."

"You appear to be a good young man. Look, my boy, listen well to what I'm going to tell you. Events are divided into official facts and facts of life. Something according to the book is an official fact. It's necessary not to mix these two kinds of truths together. Didn't I prove to you with documents that three people died?"

"Yes."

"Didn't I prove to you with receipts that I spent five hundred fifty dollars on each of the funerals?"

"Yes."

"Very well, for what stupid reason then do you kill a man with unreasonable questions? Please, my boy, if it's not too much trouble, would you bring me a glass of water? My throat's dry."

"So you're saying you have no relation to these three men who died."

"Good God Almighty! You surely don't catch on easily, brother. Listen! Get your head together and stop the nonsensical questions! Someday, if you go back to Turkey, you'll need an influential friend like me. Don't make me angry or I'll make you sorry you were born!

"Don't just stand there like an idiot! Button up your dirty jacket and behave yourself. . . ."

FLYING BIRDS

I close my eyes tight, not letting a drop of light inside. Those "no-goods" find a way to mock my game and make me miserable. I'm fed up with my eyes. I shut the bastards tight. Now, I'm in Mersin, in Pompeiopolis, in Viranşehir. I'm unshaven, my neck itches from heat and sweat. It's either July or August. Upright, white stone columns, small sand dunes, grass and brush dried in piles. Far in the distance the rustle of the Mediterranean. "Close your eyes, man, close them!" I put more pressure on my eyelids. Good, now I can hear the rustle of the sea slowly grow. You can't imagine how hot the sand is. I hop from one foot to the other on the hot sand like someone dancing to a banjo. "Keep in time, belly! Come on, keep time to this tune! It flops around like a newly caught fish. So where's the wind? Blow, damn it! It's the best time for it! You worthless wind, you blow like hell when I'm shivering in the cold, don't you? If you're going to blow, blow now! Come on, blow!"

There is a Cretan cafe on the corner of Park Avenue near Jean Talon. On Park Avenue, as far as Jean Talon, the people and buildings are very different. In this city, the tall buildings lower and broaden, the streets narrow, and the people slowly turn swarthy as you approach Jean Talon. In the same way, one hears the voice of the sea and pines while descending from the Taurus Mountains to the Mediterranean and leaving the myrtle, heather, and brambles behind. Blue eyes turn hazel, then brown. Statures shorten, hips get wider. Hair and beards grow black and thick. By the time you reach Jean Talon, you're on the Mediterranean.

Cars swish by on Park Avenue. Close your eyes, man! Again I'm on the Mediterranean viewing a beautiful Saturday noontime from the Cretan cafe. Wave after wave of people pass on the side-

Flying Birds

walk, headed for the beach. They pass by in groups, talking away. They're all angry, bickering with one another.

I order tea from the waiter. I look at the sky. It is clear as a bell. One or two white clouds in the distance. In the east, a bird appears, flying all alone. He's gallivanting around. Above him nothing, below him a torrent of people and vehicles. Below, there is no place he can perch. The bird turns left and flies off south toward the city. For an instant, the sky is empty. The swish of the cars grows. A little later I'm going to a Greek film.

Again I close my eyes tight. There's time before the movie. I return to Mersin. The Ali Kokulu Grocery! Pop-bottle cases in the shack at the rear. Then, again, the spotless sea. The newly watered earth radiates the soft smell of sun into the air. Great blue and red eyes of flowers still glow though the early afternoon sun is shadowed by clouds.

They say that the Mediterranean is dirty now. That it's stretched out like a murdered wild goat. No one can approach because of the smell and no one cares. The people are impetuous, angry, and pugnacious. They've lost the sun and everything smells of sulfur. No one walks on the beach or whistles.

I laugh and take a sip of tea. Is the sea the only one that's getting old? I wonder what happened to the young girls of those days. In the city where the brides have become grandmas, probably the sea smells like that.

I look at the sky. It's vacant. The bird that flew south can't be seen. He must be in the city. A big flock appears in the north, like a black cloud. It becomes one waving wing. Not one bird separates from the flock. They turn to the left, as one, and recede. Again they turn left. The birds are bound to each other. As one, they decide, then turn at the same instant. There is no hesitation or delay. Like trained athletes, they flap their wings in unison. One wing, two flaps, three wings, four flaps. I beat time—left, right—turn all together! They all turn together.

The bird that just flew to the city reappears. He doesn't join the flock; he flies alone. He is unconcerned about the others. The bird closes his eyes. He can't see the thousands of dirty, gassy automobiles flowing below. The city is very big. He can't fly to the wilds.

Flying Birds

He doesn't want to join the other birds who are tied to each other. He perches on a chimney, standing there like a poplar with no leaves, and turns toward the wind.

Harvey comes. "Off to the movies!" he says. While walking beside him, I look at the sky. We leave Pompeiopolis, Mersin, the Ali Kokulu, the dead Mediterranean, and head for the show.

When the lights are turned up after the movie, the place fills with screams, as if a bomb has exploded. Within two seconds, the entire audience joins in the hubbub, like a chorus. An old woman is yelling her head off. What happened? What's going on? Nobody knows. The woman wants to walk to the left. She can't go. Someone is pulling her skirt. A child wants to run. When he runs, he takes his mother's jacket with him. As the children dash about, the intensity of the screaming grows. Somehow, young men's jacket and pants buttons have been tied with thin nylon fishline to other viewers' pants and jacket buttons. When young girls begin to rise from their seats, they feel their zippers come undone and their skirts slide over their legs. The girls scream at the top of their lungs. Some invisible force is undressing them. They don't know what to yell at or whom to fight.

The man beside me is swearing like a trooper. "What son-of-a-bitch tied us together? The stupid bastards! They've tied us together like a flock of goats! If I could get my hands on them I'd know what to do! Have you ever seen the like? How could they tie this many people together without anyone's feeling it?"

The guy's friend says, "Forget it! Enjoy yourself! You don't see a party like this every day. Look at all these jackasses around us. Enjoy a good laugh!"

On the seventh row, a woman wearing a fur coat has her wig fly off, leaving her head as bare as a cue ball. The wig is caught on the jacket button of the man beside her. In order to save her wig, she turns to the left, which pulls the skirt of someone on her other side. The skirt flies off and the woman raises hell. So on both sides there are two "baldies." A horrible catastrophe. What "lowdown" has done this?

After two or three minutes, things calm down a little. Eyes become accustomed to the light, revealing this scene: Nearly a hundred men, women, and children in the theater have been tied to others in the audience by thin nylon line. When one moves, someone else's coat, pants, or skirt is pulled with them.

At this point, two young girls are skirtless. One pretends it is unimportant; she forgot to wear panties.

After the panic passes, the noise subsides a little but talking continues. Two well-dressed women sitting in the fourth row regard a shabbily dressed woman beside them. "Just look at this woman," they mutter to each other. "Imagine them tying us to this dirty thing. We wouldn't even use her as a maid!" On the sixth row, a girl complains, "Damn them! With all these handsome men here in the movie, they tie me to this bum with dirty fingernails. If my father finds out, I'll be shamed!" A young boy is crying, "Mama, I have to go peepee!"

A sharp whistle shrills. Two policemen appear on the stage. The audience suddenly becomes silent. One could hear a pin drop. Over the speaker a voice says, "Break the lines holding you and quietly go out!" But the audience, which has become used to being tied, doesn't want to stop the fun and ignores the order. The people holler, yell, and increase the commotion.

Most laugh but some are angry. When they come outside, some are still tied together.

I look up at the sky to see if the birds are still flying as a flock.

ROOTS

I decided to learn who my forefathers were. Some fellow did a lot of research, discovered his ancestors came from Africa as Negro slaves, and wrote a book about it. He became a celebrity overnight.

Big deal! If I'd been black, I would have deduced immediately that my ancestors were slaves from Africa. What is there to discover about that? How could a man be as black as coal and claim to come from Europe, for hell's sale! He's in no position to say he's German, French, or English. A black living in America undoubtedly would be an African black, plain as two plus two equals four! That's all there is to it! The writer of the book overemphasized the troubles of the blacks. He made his story very touching. The reader thinks of the blacks and says, "Those poor people!" I say, "What's done is done! Take care of today and stop beating a dead horse!" But nobody listens. They all take the easy way out and blame their white ancestors.

I saw that searching for roots was pleasant and also profitable, so I decided to look for my own. I read a bunch of books and studied old registers. The clues that turned up were absolutely amazing. However, I was able to go back no further than seven generations. It's a known fact that my family came into existence in Anatolia. Certain differences in the physical attributes of our family members showed that we didn't spring from the same roots as other people. Later on, experiments in the university laboratory tied me directly to the first human.

Don't think that I'm boasting about being Adam's little grandson. I can now state definitely that before God created Adam, He created another creature. True, all the holy books and the theologians claim that the human race began with Adam, but this theory is not a fact. Another species existed before Adam, who appeared on earth later. Therefore, it was this creature who suffered the first trials and tribulations of the world. By the time Adam was created, everything had been prepared. Every kind of plant and animal flourished on the earth—a complete, a perfect world. How sweet it was! No winter, no summer! Neither heat nor cold! Rivers flowed with milk and honey. Trees were loaded with quince, apples, pears, flowers, cherries . . . One might gather and eat all he wanted!

But life wasn't that easy for the first creature. Furthermore, that first creature was not as idiotic as Adam. If *he* had been living in such plenty, he never would have struggled with God and been banished from the heavenly garden. Well, this first creature was my ancestor. I can say this definitely: I don't think an idiot like Adam can be found in our family tree.

Let's consider my great-grandfather, Yusuf. This grandfather tasted an apple but three times in his entire life. He even shared his tiny field, that he worked by hand, with three partners. In his forty-year life, he could never remember going to bed with a full belly, not even once. I don't think Yusuf was stupid enough to go against God and get thrown out of heaven. I carried out my research buoyed up by this fact.

God created a barren Anatolia before he created this circus. The adventure of Anatolian civilization wasn't all that easy. Obviously, our family wasn't created with the prospects of a life filled with plenty. Excavations show that the first creatures lived in a place in the sky about three hundred kilometers above where Anatolia is today. Inscriptions remain from that period showing that God produced this first creature even before He created the earth and filled the void with air. Due to His not being used to such work, it appears that His first creature was fashioned rather amateurishly. He didn't bestow upon him a complete set of organs. It's obvious that this first creation was not well thought out, planned, nor executed. I believe He couldn't easily foresee the possibility that this being might have good intentions. Inscriptions relate the story of this creature as follows:

"He opened his eyes to a void. When he couldn't find anyplace around him to place his feet or walk, he just hung there in all his nakedness in thin air. He didn't know what to do. All was emptiness. Either from ignorance or from forgetfulness, God had not created anyplace for the naked Anatolian to put his feet. When the poor creature started to swim in those depths of darkness, a great sadness lodged in his heart. Thus the first feeling he learned was 'Melancholy.' Then hunger. He couldn't eat because food had not yet been created. Thus he learned 'Hunger.' After more time had passed, he became tired of being suspended there. And when he could find no place to rest or set foot, he learned 'Fatigue.'"

Wall inscriptions end the interesting story here. What happened to this creature with no world? I don't know. It's certain he didn't die, but I couldn't find any information concerning his life from any other source.

When one compares this living being's story with Adam's, there are many similarities, yet there also are great differences in their characters. Adam appears to be an opportunistic, lazy, and spoiled being. He wants to control everything. In addition, he exhibits warrior-like tendencies. Subsequently, we observe that in consonance with these tendencies, he forms his concepts of heroism, bravery, and aggression.

As for that first creature, he was passive and addicted to creature comforts.

Further scientific digs revealed more details in the story of the Anatolian, which follow:

After a long period, just as the first creature was becoming accustomed to nothingness, hunger, and darkness, God appeared to him again. The first human, unaware of His greatness, power, and oneness, was very pleased when he beheld this being who resembled himself.

"Are you also alone, as I am?" he asked. "I don't know what evil-intentioned person brought us here. If only I can get my hands on him! He's in big trouble with me!"

God was displeased with this forthright statement. In a deep voice he thundered:

"I am God!"

The creature, unaware of the real meaning of this, answered: "Pleased to meet you! If you want the truth, I thought I was alone.

It's nice that you're with me. I'm sorry I can't introduce myself to you because I don't know what I am. Had I known, I would have told you. So your name's God?"

"No, it's not my name. I myself *am* God."

"What's the difference?"

"What's the difference? You're merely a creation. *I'm* the one who creates. You must bow down to me with respect."

The creature looked at God in astonishment.

"Until this moment I didn't know what I was," he said. "How did you learn this?"

"I know everything," He replied, "because I created you."

The first creature, who understood now that the being facing him was God, asked: "Why did you create and place me in such an imperfect environment? You gave me feet but no field to walk in. You gave me a mouth but nothing to eat, eyes but no nature to see. You gave me reason but nothing to reason about. You gave me a heart and left me without love."

In a sad voice God answered: "You're absolutely right. I'll create a field for you to stand in and, for your feet, land to endlessly walk on. For your mouth, I will first give nourishment, then the ability to talk. I will grant to your intelligence, thinking. This will be a little difficult getting used to. You will not believe believable things. Unbelievable things you will call ordinary. For example, a round world for you!"

The creature looked sourly at the world that appeared before him:

"It's obvious you never created a world before. How can I walk on such a body?"

If the text is true, the Anatolian creature did have a lot of trouble standing on his feet on the world. Every time he stood up, he rolled back down like a child trying to stand on a round rubber ball. After rather a long period of time, the Anatolian mastered standing on his feet. When he succeeded in walking and running on a round world like an acrobat, he experimented with putting his surroundings in order.

At this point God returned. He took the globe under the Anatolian in his hand and spun it like a top. When the ball beneath him spun like a top, the Anatolian again fell on his ass.

So that's the interesting story of how my first ancestor began.

MUD

The old Indian squatted beneath Orford Mountain like a yellow, wrinkled leaf. The deep lines on his face moved in the blowing wind; they deepened. His eyes were as rheumy as a drunk's, sticky white. He was crushed to the mountain slope like an overloaded camel. He hadn't the strength to move; the Indian was pulp.

"We're no longer friends!" he moaned.

Not friends? Not friends with whom? Whom was he angry with? His face was utterly confused, a garden after the storm, uprooted, disorganized. Without looking up, he muttered:

"Every year it gets a little steeper, longer, bigger, and more precipitous. It's going, becoming my enemy and taking the food from my hand. It will strangle me. It waits in ambush on my path."

I wanted to ask who, but remained silent.

"Every year, a little more escapes me, torments me. It used to be right under my nose. Morning and evening, I was on its back. It was my horse. I reared with it. Now I can no longer see its head. Was that all that grew steeper, more precipitous? No, it was the same with all the birds, rabbits, and deer. I can't catch any of them. They left me here alone on the slopes and went away. They used to give me fresh, clear, cool water. I had a wind that dried my sweat. Now it's become a desert. It doesn't want me. It made the near, distant. It made the easy, difficult. I don't know why it's angry. My love lacked for nothing. I sang her songs. I spoke with her on the peaks. I listened to the talking of the wind on the heights. I gazed with love and excitement. I knew her as homeland, mother, heart. I was sad at her growing old; when her soil flowed, I built a dike and protected her. She rejected me, grew steep and precipitous. She didn't want me on her. She wouldn't let me pass. She took the strength from my legs and struck me to the ground."

In the morning's first light, the azure lake was a patchwork of color. The sun warmed, raised, and swelled it like fresh dough. A morning fog shrank the mountain and narrowed it. I squatted beside the Indian. He continued his monologue:

"My ancestors used to say, 'When the wet soap slips through your hand, it opens the door to other pastures.' My life is slipping from my hand. My day must be coming. Everything is cramped and shriveled."

"Hello!" I said.

This Indian, named "Darkness," smiled.

"Who's the enemy running from you?" I asked.

"The mountain," he answered, "the air, sun, water!"

"This mountain? That sun in the sky? This water? This air?" I asked.

"Is there any other mountain or sun here?"

Then he continued his murmuring:

"Look, in the old days the sun cascaded his rays like a horse's tail. Water and light splashed down the mountains. The light called, the sun shone on everything. Fresh almond perfume filled the air. The sharp smell of green grass, wild flowers, and blackberries became fog and covered all the highlands. A man wandered the mountains in the harsh smell, like a fish who created water. There were pears and apples. The rain of love was juicy. There were lettuce and cabbages. Love was green. Now all beauty has been destroyed—or else I can't see and feel it. There were mountain blackberry bushes in the wilds, on the slopes. When they scratched, the sun filled a person's mouth. Spring water flowed in. You were refreshed. Your heart was filled with sun and spring. Honey flowers have gone from my smell leaving only the nose behind, dirty, wrinkled, runny.

"When the junipers and pines see me, they no longer release their spring perfumes, they no longer set free the mountain air. In the old days, the sun-smelling tomatoes were my friend. My hands smelled green when I touched the tomato leaves in the sun. The smell of apples and pears used to be wind for the slopes when I came. Everything's lost! It's ended!

Mud

"In the old days there were colors in fire, in tulips. The cantaloupe-yellow, the melon-red of roses played in the sun. In the mountain mists, the cool blue turned to green in the sun. The steamy mountain was a purple lilac. At noon, the sun was a canary in blue water. All colors have flown away! Now all is gray, black, dirty.

"Sleep must be coming. My forefathers used to say, 'When the great sleep draws near, smells diminish, mountains steepen, birds quiet, roads lengthen, bread gets harder, and the wind gets harsh.'

"Truly, the great sleep must be coming. Everyone's against me. Everyone speaks in a low voice. Everyone has secrets. The breeze doesn't rustle the leaves anymore, even if it blows. All birds are silent. There used to be more birds than apples in these trees. There was more red than black. There was more sound than silence. The place twittered like a spring splashing down the rocks. I listened to the voice of birds in the pouring rain. The night rustle of the mountain told of bursting buds. Everything has stopped, everything has been extinguished."

"Many things haven't changed," I said. "Everything has the same beauty. Come, let me take you to the park. Listen to the birds there. Look at the flowers there."

"You're young, that's why," he replied. "Color seems different to the young. Sound is heard differently."

"No, it isn't, come and see!"

"Impossible! Soil and water turn to mud in man's hand. The color in the park isn't mountain color! The sound in the park isn't bird songs!"

A bystander said, "Leave him. He's a crazy Indian!"

I left the old Indian and returned to the village. Five years ago we had run away from the plague, the city, and come to this village. Here in the highlands of Orford we'd spent our summer vacation on the lakeshore.

The following morning, upon awakening, I left the house early. I wanted to see my surroundings. It was an old village. The sun left a mark where it rose, a red light. The small lake at the foot of the mountain was patched with a thousand colors. In the smoky distance, houses glowed. As I walked, I thought of what the Indian had said. The years *had* shrunk the area, faded the colors, and dulled the sounds. When I focused on it, I was aware that the opposite shore had become a little more distant. And the houses seemed a little farther away this year. White, rose-melon-roofed houses on the opposite shore had turned to spots. Previously, the far shore had been filled with lemon-bloom-faced houses. Now it was a long white blur. Windy pines filled the space between the confused white areas. Before me, the triangular, ice-cream-cone Orford Mountain with its white flowers had become distant from the village. The pines covering the mountain had become smaller, dusty green, and hazy.

Listening to myself, I walked along the green grassy path with yellow and pink on both sides. In the sharp silence, the sound of cattle, the first wood fires in the darkness were clear and distinct, ripping air and water. At noon the lake came alive. The sky became vibrant. The freshness of the trees and flowers disappeared. Colors dissipated and faded. Sounds disappeared, erased in the fog. The lake was transformed into a marketplace, took on color, yellowed, glowed purple and red. When the sun struck the mountains, boulders fell into the water. Childhood and youth flew away. A mound of light, smelling of ripe quince, set fire to the lake, then the grass.

For an instant, I seemed to remember the past five years; I almost grasped them. Then, again, the circle moved on.

MORNING TRAFFIC

The city's morning traffic flowed along the underground road like sewage, fast, two ways. Aboveground, pink started to mix with gray. Morning, from the east, poured like urine on the dirty snow. Sunlight spread.

Osman must be where I left him twenty-five years ago. The last time I saw him, he was standing on the shore throwing stones into the Mediterranean. The June sun appeared where the water turned to white.

When I asked, "What are you doing, Osman?" this boy from Kilis answered, "I'm filling the sea." I looked at him in amazement as he laughed at the sea.

"Osman," I said, "you can't fill the sea by throwing stones, can you?" He smiled at me. "One can fill it with patience, not stones."

Osman must still be throwing stones. He was a patient person.

Moans rose from the machines being tortured, along with the mechanical hum of steel gears and the smells of rust, gas, fuel oil, and sulfur, from the vehicles flowing under the city.

The city's foundation was alive. It stirred like ants attacking a bug. Tracks were turning, the city moving when the hand of the clock touched six.

Osman came within a hairsbreadth of living a life of ease, bird-free, mule-stubborn, and donkey-lazy. He had in the palm of his hand a happy life, living off others, beholden to no one. But city life wiped Osman out; the well went dry. The city made him a well-fed, little man.

The sun, an image appearing for an instant in a mirror, shone like silver in the sky. In Place D'Armes, it became light at the base of a wall or two. Puke-green empty beer cans sparkled in the snow. Church bells moaned in the graveyard wind.

When I closed my eyes, I saw Osman on the shore at the edge of the blue water; birds in the sky, a shore filled with people yelling, singing.

"Since morning, this sea has come and gone three thousand times," Osman said.

"Did you count?" I asked.

"No my friend! I'm learning, I'm learning to be the sea. I can come and go now. If I can only become blue, I'll be a perfect sea."

From the road, a split in the earth dividing the city in two, the rising sounds slowly spread from west to east like a flood. They dulled and silenced other noises.

Every four minutes, like gas gushing from a cave in the ground, a double line of people thirty meters long came out. In the narrow streets, the giant earthworm advanced silently and divided. The subway trains were vomiting their green-hued people on the streets.

In the month of January, Place D'Armes remained buried in dead snow. Colorless and viscous, the snow resembled dog dung and smelled like a carcass. The flowing flood of people trudged through the slushy dung. As the pedestrians walked side by side, their heads were bowed, their mouths silent.

I found Osman singing a lullaby on the shore. I asked, "Are you trying to sing yourself to sleep?" He replied, "No, I'm putting the sea to sleep. I've been singing this lullaby for three hours. One end of the sea sleeps; see, the wind stopped. The candle in the sky has gone out." When Osman opened his mouth, the sea rustled in a person's ears.

The wind blew like a long sword and cut the pedestrians' faces in two. Big, red, frozen noses, summer eggplants scattered to the ground. No one stopped; they kept on going.

Jobholders came from the suburbs and slowly filled the vacuum in the city. At nine o'clock, the whole city was full. First the narrow-shouldered, then the small-headed, and finally the other jobholders arrived. Row on row they took their places inside the cogs in the meat grinder.

A hard wind blew. One of the pedestrians coughed. The whole row coughed.

A man with a swollen drunkard's nose stood on the corner. He was both poor and drunk. Inside his oily-collared overcoat he was warm, in spring. He was looking mockingly and bitterly at the passersby.

"Look at you jackasses!" he said to the file of people before him. "Even cattle on their way to the slaughterhouse aren't as complaisant as you."

This man must be one of us. He resembled Osman a little.

Unconcerned as a farmhand cursing in the fields, the walking people flowed past the drunk, like a train of freight cars.

No one showed the slightest interest. The drunk got angrier. Moaning came from the underground automobile subways. The city was howling. Ambulances, fire engines, were flying along screaming and moaning. When the drunk heard the monstrous horns he laughed. His dirty black rotten teeth shone in the pink sunshine.

"Great!" he said, "the bastards. So you're on fire! Burn, you bastards. If your butts are singed you won't turn around and put out the fire." Then he took a small harmonica from his pocket and started to play.

Within a few minutes, the sky turned black. The building on the corner was burning and coloring its surroundings.

Before I came, I found Osman on the watermelon-red seashore. From a well on the shore, he was carrying bucket after bucket of water to the sea. "What's up?" I asked. "The sea's on fire, I have to put it out. I've been working on it for three hours." The sun was going down. I laughed at Osman; he laughed, too. If he wanted to, he could burn the sea.

A policeman wearing white gloves told the line of pedestrians, "Please take another street." He changed the path of the line. They disappeared in the dirty snow among the buildings.

I said to a man standing beside me, "Let's go watch the fire." He answered, "Forget it, we can see it better on TV tonight."